A SPIRIT

The Greatest Change of All

Lynn Telford-Sahl

Living In Balance Publications
Modesto, CA

The Greatest Change of All

Copyright © 1999 by Lynn Telford-Sahl

Published by Living in Balance Publications
1700 McHenry Ave. Ste. 65-B
Modesto, CA 95350

Cover design by Lightbourne Images © 1998
Artwork title: *Circle of Friends, Fine Friends, Love and Support*
Artist: Gina Designs

Library of Congress Catalog Card Number 98-091760

ISBN 0-9667148-7-3

Printed in the United States of America

True Self

Hidden in thoughtful recesses,
cloudy fear like the night wind banishing the moon.
Seeking to emerge from inner depths
to dance—call out,
not quietly, not softly like the good girl
but impolitely and growing louder, brighter,
whirling dervishly into her gypsy future
into her one and ravishing true Self,
reclaiming, moving, writing, screaming,
being. . . yes.

Lynn Telford-Sahl

I dedicate this book to my mom, Barbara: You left too soon, but your belief in me and your unconditional love helped me become the woman I am today—And to my grandmother, Laila: Without your zest for life, creativity and total support during my hellish years, I wouldn't be.

Acknowledgments

I give praise and gratitude to the three editors who held my hand and provided invaluable editorial support, each in their unique and gifted manner.

To Val Hillsdon-Hutton: Who took the very rough first draft and transformed it into readable form.

To Kim Kelly: My dear literary cousin, friend and gifted horsewoman, who spent many, many hours fine-tuning the manuscript to get it to the next level. I am indebted to you for life.

To Jennifer Grainger: Her eye for detail and persistence in convincing me to keep at the first chapter and for all her consulting support.

To all women in my matriarchal family who believe women are incredible, wonderful and most of all, equal.

To Lane, sister, gifted writer, inspired thinker, unafraid to be her own unique self. Thank-you for staying.

To the men in my family, who are gentle, kind, loving, and believe in their women and children—especially my son, Rich, recent Paint Ball World Champ, who doesn't always "get" his wacky mom, but totally loves and supports her nonetheless.

And to Dave, my husband, who has blessed me with his support and enthusiasm, humor and love, I am grateful every day.

Chapter 1

Leaning into the hot, dry wind whipping up the cliff, I was standing on launch. The taste of fear was in my throat and my heart was pounding. . . hard. "Breathe," I repeated to myself. "Breathe." Buying a few extra moments, my trembling hands reached up to adjust the rubber band holding my straight blonde hair in its unaccustomed pony tail. Forty-five is too young to die, I thought, but there was no turning back now.

Wally, my tandem hang gliding partner yelled, "One, two, three, ready!" My cue to run like hell—off the edge. At 5' 9" Wally is just a few inches taller than I am but his strong, gym-trained body has all the strength needed to launch us off the cliff. No time to balk now. I ran. . . stumbled. . . he dragged me the rest of the way and finally the wind lifted us and we were airborne.

"Taylor," shouted Wally over the snap of the wind, "get into your harness, now!" Fumbling to get my legs into the harness flapping around me, I looked down. "Oh my God," I gasped. "I'm flying!"

Watching me struggle to catch my breath, Wally shouted, "You're not going to throw up, are you?"

"Hope not," I squeaked back, finding my voice. But I was none too sure.

My lower back throbbed, every muscle strained and tight, as if the tension would somehow keep me safe. With nothing holding my body but the two inch wide strap tied to the glider, I had to trust Wally's skill as a pilot as I faced my lifelong terror of heights. I tried to relax and take in the panoramic view of the valley below. Glimpses of oak tree leaves, painted Indian Summer orange and brown, rushed by. Mostly though I was in shock and my mind would not let in the full beauty of the fall scenery.

Fifteen minutes later Wally told me to pull my legs out of my harness and get ready to land. The ground rushed up at us unbelievably fast and again Wally had to drag me as I ran to keep up with him. The adrenaline pumping through my body made me feel weak and nauseous and my legs rubbery. Yet my mind registered what I had accomplished. "I did it! I actually did it!" I felt high for hours afterwards. I can still barely believe I voluntarily leaped off that cliff to face my fear.

I shook my head in an effort to return to the present as I eased my sporty, silver Camaro to the curb in front of Rebecca's white on white, expansive ranch style home. The fall sun was beginning to set above the heavy shake roof. Butterflies were flitting about in my stomach as I thought about the telling the "girls" about my flight. Ranging in age from thirty-eight to fifty we're not exactly girls, but girlfriends is what we six friends call ourselves, acknowledging the bond we have formed over the past three years. Once a month on Thursday I finish my appointments early so I can make it to our group gathering. . . it's what keeps me sane.

Headlights flashed behind me as Veronica raced the engine of her old Porsche, shiny green and spotless from her regular care. It's her baby and one of the few luxuries she allows herself.

Veronica pushed open her car door, wearily climbing out. She looked more drawn than usual. Her face revealed the stress of attending to the needs of thirty or more patients a day in her busy medical practice. "God, what a week I've had!" she said, pushing the brown wispy bangs off her forehead, something she did so often she now sported a cowlick. "Oh this hair!" Veronica didn't complain much, except about her thin flyaway brown hair. Despite the dark circles of fatigue under her eyes, and the sag to her normally straight posture, she still looked years younger than forty-eight.

"You O.K.?" I slipped my arm through hers as we walked past the white petunias lining the pristine walkway leading to the dark wood-stained double entry doors. She smiled wearily. "I'm just so glad to be here. After twelve hours of listening to patients' complaints, I need my girlfriends."

The front door burst open. "Well, it's about time!" Rebecca's huge smile leaked all the way up into her round blue eyes, and the skin around them was crinkled from much use. A classic beauty with streaked blonde hair and large shapely mouth, it's hard to believe Rebecca just celebrated her fiftieth birthday making her the oldest of our group. A therapist like I am, Rebecca specializes in school counseling and has a small private practice while I focus on addiction issues. She hugged us both, and we headed toward the laughter in the living room.

Gloria, tall and well-shaped, posed in the doorway. Her left hand was resting gracefully on the molding around the door, showing off her sparkly diamond tennis bracelet, a symbol of her former financial security. She swung around taking in the admiring looks at her trim, supple body. Her face lit up. "Taylor, Veronica, you're here!" She threw her strong arms around me in a powerful bear hug, then did the same to Veronica.

"Gloria, you look great. . . as usual," I said, disengaging myself. Gloria and I had grown up together. We lived across the street from each other from age twelve through our first year of high school. Recently divorced she's directed her serious commitment to fitness into a new career as a personal trainer. As she approaches forty-five, she's re-thinking her life and it's one of the reasons she never misses our meetings. I can't imagine my life without Gloria in it.

"Hey, Taylor," Linda said, laughing in the innocent, open manner that endears her to her friends. Her oversized bright blue tee shirt can't successfully conceal her thirty-eight DD chest size. She always wears pants a little large to add bulk to her narrow hips. "We've all been waiting for you." Linda, thirty-eight, was in the midst of an early mid-life crisis centered around giving to herself rather than everyone else. She'd reported on previous evenings, every time she tried to think of herself first, she felt horribly guilty. She felt she was flunking therapy because she wasn't making much progress. "We're dying to hear about the flight. I can't believe you did that." Her wild, multi-colored beaded earrings swung crazily as she grabbed my arm.

I gave her a quick hug. "On my way over, I was having deep thoughts about my flight, and that ever present feeling—fear." She nodded. We headed over to the couch and sat down, as Donna joined us. She'd already made herself comfortable, her navy suit jacket tossed casually on the couch behind her, the top button of her skirt undone, releasing the strain of having to hold in her bulging abdomen.

"My monthly oasis!" Donna said, with a sigh. "No clients, just me and my girlfriends." Her never lipsticked mouth parted in a full smile revealing a little gap between her front teeth that her parents were unhappy about after years of childhood braces. She reached into the candy dish in the middle of the coffee table, grabbed a red foil-wrapped kiss, unwrapped it and popped it into her mouth. A grateful smile spread over her face.

Linda and I laughed, watching her—Donna does love her chocolate. Divorced, after a short unhappy marriage in her twenties, she wonders if there's something wrong with her because she enjoys being single. Donna is adopted and isn't close to her family. She doesn't have children. The group has become her family. Large boned and heavier than she'd like to be, she's always fighting her weight, but just can't lay off the candy. She popped another one into her mouth. "Chocolate's not the main reason I come to our meetings, but it's definitely a good one," she said.

"I think it probably *is* the main reason you come," I laughed. "It's not like you're coming for the spiritual stuff." Donna doesn't believe in God, religion or metaphysics, but she's not sure it's all crazy either. She plays the devil's advocate in our group.

Gloria's curly reddish hair hung just to her beautifully defined muscular shoulders, the result of the last two years obsessive attention to fitness. She walked over. "Hey Donna, leave some for me, O.K.?" She slipped her arm around Donna's ample waist and squeezed her. Donna stuck her tongue out at her as she wrapped her lips around one more kiss, and said, "It's hard to believe we've been coming here for three years. Remember our first try?"

"Yeah, a great idea, but not the right time," Linda said. Her dark hair is a perfect frame for her startling blue eyes. Her crooked nose keeps her from being a classic beauty, but Linda is something. All the men adore her, but she's happily married with two teenage kids, and can't be bothered with the attention. "After we put the word out, we had at least twenty women and a couple of men."

Rebecca stood with her arms crossed over her chest. "I thought we'd be talking about healing techniques, herbs and stuff like that," she said grimacing. "When the men joined, they stuck together and then so did the women and then we all quit going."

"I wasn't all that surprised," I admitted. "It made me mad though. Typical of how men want to create structure, ruining our easy flow with their need to organize and control. And, we just let them take over."

Gloria, majored in drama in high school. She loved being dramatic and threw her arms in the air. "But now we're back, we're great and we decide how we want our meetings to go!"

"Yeah!" someone said as laughter filled the room.

I stepped back into myself. I do that a lot. Just sort of fade out. I mean, I'm still in the room and I'll smile and nod at the right time, but I'm not really there. I'm here, inside me—looking and listening. I'm warm and safe and comfortable with this group of women. We're all so different, but we share a common bond of friendship and spiritual connection.

Rebecca is the wit of the group, keeps us in stitches because she considers nothing sacred and jokes about the upper-class women she associates with, as well as about herself. I looked at her across the room, laughing as usual, her blonde hair catching the light as she indulged her chocolate craving. She's always practiced strictly traditional therapy, but is beginning to explore holistic avenues. It's been a real leap for her.

And there's Linda, who's worked so hard to find out who she is this last year. She's struggling to let the psychic part of herself out and at the same time balance her massage practice with the husband she adores, her sixteen year old daughter and thirteen year old son.

And, of course, Donna. She practices family law and is so smart, it's scary. She thinks spirituality is for the birds. Though she thinks she's too heavy, I like her larger body style and think she looks perfect. She's a challenging addition and having a critic in the group keeps us from taking ourselves too seriously.

I came back to the room. Tonight, I had an ulterior motive for being here. I reached into my bag and pulled out a slightly crumpled, bright pink sheet of paper with bold black lettering: **THE GREATEST CHANGE OF ALL**. Everyone except Donna grabbed their own copies off tables and out of purses. I was stunned. We all belong to different professional organizations, so we rarely get the same flyers in the mail.

"What's it mean?" Rebecca asked. She's always looking for spiritual signs and her eyes sparkled. This was one for sure.

"Oh, wow, this is like too weird," Donna said in a mocking, spooky voice. Ever the non-believer.

"Well, it is a little strange," I admitted. "I mean, how often do we all get the same stuff in the mail and why did we all bring it to group? I for one, was so excited and I don't know, charged, when I first got it that I got a stomach ache!" Except for Donna, we agreed we felt something powerful in this flyer. Ever since my hang gliding trial by fire, I'd been searching for something to help me understand what happened to me.

"Anyone interested in going?" I asked. We all looked at the flyer again, then at each other.

"I wonder what it means, 'The Greatest Change of All'. It's pretty vague, don't you think?" Linda said, pointing to the title.

"Sounds grandiose to me," Veronica said.

"Probably about menopause," laughed Rebecca. "Every woman I know is going through *that* change."

"Speak for yourself," Donna said and Linda nodded.

"Listen you guys," I interrupted. "I need to share something—and it has to do with this damned flyer." The urgency in my voice caused all the women to quiet down and look at me expectantly.

I took a deep breath and let it out slowly. "I've got all these thoughts and feelings stirring inside from my flight and this incredible dream I had the other night. I think it's related to these changes going on inside me and why it's important to go to this retreat. You know how sometimes when you're dreaming you know you're dreaming?" Nods all around. "O.K., well, I'd been having my usual insomnia, you know, the 3:00 a.m. wake-up call? When I finally got back to sleep, I knew I was dreaming, but I felt awake and I was floating. . . flying over trees and looking down at my neighborhood. I was light and happy and calm. I saw an old man walking under me with his head bowed and his shoulders slumped. I flew closer and hovered above him. I had to help him, but I knew that I couldn't do it alone. I prayed to the angelic helpers, God, Goddess, All That Is and everyone I could think of. I even remembered *A Course In Miracles* and what I'd learned about miracles happening for our highest good.

"A brilliant white light engulfed him and he changed completely. He stood up straight, his head came up and he smiled. I don't know exactly what happened, but my heart exploded. I knew that I could help others. Then I woke up. I still felt soft and light and dreamy and filled with bliss. I felt like I imagine a holy person might feel when he channels love. No fear. . . just a deep peace. That feeling stayed with me all day. I wish I could have had that kind of trust when I ran off that cliff."

I stopped and looked around. The girls were staring at me—all attention. "I want more bliss, less fear and a deeper spiritual connection in my life. I think this retreat for The Greatest Change might be the ticket," I finished.

Rebecca broke the thoughtful silence. "Do you really think it's possible to live in bliss all the time?"

I shrugged. "I want to believe it is. My mind says it's unrealistic. My heart says it's definitely possible. Who knows? Maybe the true reality is somewhere in between. I don't know, but I want to find out."

Gloria picked up a kiss and put it down again. The wrappers of the two chocolates she'd allowed herself, neatly in front of her. "Well, I know what bliss is for me—eating. That's why I got into personal training. I love showing others how to manage their weight and fitness. It gives me a satisfied feeling and helps to remind me to be aware of what I put into my mouth. Is that what you mean? That happy, content, satisfied feeling?"

I nodded. "I think bliss is just that. I don't know how, but I want to create more of the feelings from my dream in my daily life and something keeps telling me that this retreat is the key."

Linda leaned forward, anxiety showing in her blue eyes. "Some of you have gone away for weekends together, but we've never gone as a whole group. I'm afraid my family wouldn't be able to get along without me if I went away for a weekend, much less a whole week."

Veronica hadn't said a word until now. She was often quiet, but she missed nothing. "Tell us about your flight Taylor." Her eyes narrowed into her look of concentration.

I nodded. "I remember breathing and running and then nothing. I'm embarrassed to admit this, but I passed out for a few seconds. If I hadn't visualized and prepared for weeks before I wouldn't have been able to do it at all. But I was caught off guard by the intensity of the fear."

Donna loudly said, "Taylor, you're either very brave or crazy!"

"Both probably. The flight changed my life. Facing my fear of heights and pushing through it was really hard. But, I knew if I didn't do it, I'd be letting myself down."

Veronica's intense gaze was still upon me. "We're all in some kind of change process, aren't we? Personally and professionally, the foundations are shifting. But, we're a constant for each other. No wonder we love our group so much."

We sat quietly for a moment, thinking.

Gloria, succumbing to her third chocolate said, "I have this new business I'm doing. It's a huge risk. No health insurance, company benefits, or regular paycheck. The no paycheck is the scariest part."

"What is it about change that's so threatening?" Rebecca asked.

"I find it exciting. If everything stays the same, it's boring! Maybe you just like to be comfortable too much," prodded Donna, ever the different voice.

"Well, there's comfort and there's terror. Some of us are making leaps that are so different it really forces us to stretch," I said.

"It's not just the many changes going on in my life and the world, but how fast things are changing," said Linda looking again at the flyer in her hand. "It's hard to keep up. Makes me wonder how this retreat on change could help me. I wish I wasn't so afraid to leave my family." Her cheeks reddened in embarrassment. "I mean, I'm 38 years old, for God's sake!"

"Sometimes it doesn't feel like we've made a lot of progress, but anyone remember where women were twenty years ago? We made 69 cents on the dollar and there *was* no glass ceiling for women executives to bump up against," I reminded my friends.

"I remember girls in college who would do almost anything to get the right guy. And, if I had something planned with a girlfriend and a guy called for a date, I got dumped. I hated all the competition," Rebecca frowned.

"Well, the only reason women competed with you Rebecca is because you're so damned gorgeous, they were all jealous!" I said, shaking my finger at her. Rebecca was tall, blonde, beautiful and a delight to be around. We all loved her. "I think women compete with each other because we're socialized to think we have to. It's so stupid. If our partners are going to leave us for another woman, they'll do it whether we have true women friends or not. As some great philosopher once said, 'Men come and go, but a friend is a friend forever'."

I looked at my wristwatch. Two hours had flown by. "Anyone want to get coffee and talk some more? I'm hungry."

"You're always hungry," Rebecca chided me. She and Veronica agreed to join me. We said our good-byes, promising to touch bases again about the retreat. We decided on an espresso cafe not too far from Rebecca's house. Veronica arrived first, gunning her Porsche as usual. She grabbed a table by the window, and I slid in across from her.

Rebecca threw her purse down, and sat next to me. We all decided on desserts. Our waitress was young and flustered. Her once white apron was covered with stains—the aftermath of a very long day. When she left, I started right in.

"A few years ago, I got a notice about a Native American women's retreat. I went because I felt compelled, and the pull for the 'Greatest Change' is even stronger." I held up my hands. "I know I'm always telling you guys about my weird intuitive feelings, but I really do believe it's more than coincidence that we all got the same flyer and brought it to group tonight." Our desserts arrived with three clanks as the waitress slid the plates across the table.

"Can I get you anything else?" she asked. We shook our heads and she scurried off.

I took a bite of my apple crisp. Heaven. "A few years ago if someone had said the word 'psychic,' I'd have thought more psycho than metaphysical. I remember my husband and sister sitting around our kitchen table fifteen years ago, talking about their weird intuitions and metaphysical experiences, I just tuned them out." I looked off into the room for a minute. "Part of the change we're all going through is our spirituality, isn't it?"

"Yes," Veronica said, slicing off a corner of a gooey, chocolate piece of cake. "I was raised Catholic, but I never did buy it. I was in limbo for a long time. I think I replaced the Church with science, and I love being a doctor, but in the last five years I've felt my connection to spirit again. . . here," she pointed to her heart and wiped frosting off her lips. "That's why I love nature. My spiritual base is in the mountains. Mostly the Mount Shasta area. Besides, there's a whole bunch of spiritual seekers, artists and naturalists there, so I never feel like an oddball."

I touched her arm. "I know what you mean Veronica." I really did too. This woman had come a long way in her spiritual journey in just a few years. "I didn't have any connection to spirituality growing up either. I was an atheist until about ten years ago. I mean, my mom and my aunt didn't believe, and they raised me, so why should I? My grandmother's Christian Science beliefs must have stuck in my head, though, and that's probably why I started exploring the spiritual part of myself." I stopped. It still hurts to talk about my mother and grandmother.

"How long has it been, Taylor?" Rebecca asked.

I closed my eyes for a moment. "Two years. They went so fast. . . within seven weeks of each other. No time to prepare, really. I was so close to my mother's mother, Grandma Laila. She was there for me when I was a kid.

She never forced her religion on me and she was practical. She always saw the best in me and helped me see it also."

Veronica had finished her cake, and after I licked the back of my fork, I pushed my plate aside also. Rebecca hadn't said a word, and was looking down at her coffee cup. I couldn't stop talking. "My mother told me a few years before she died that when she was a child, she believed in fairies. I'll never forget that." I took a sip of coffee. "Why did she stop believing? Why do any of us stop believing in mystery?"

"Hey," Rebecca said. "The western world is so intellectual, it's amazing any of us can hold on to faith."

"Anyway," I laughed, a bit shaky, but it lightened the mood. "I just started to wonder if there really is a God, and what believing in God means? What if there really was something other than this physical world? What do people who believe in something beyond this do every day?" This is what always happens when we start talking. We feed each other's excitement, then we can't stop talking.

Rebecca laughed, and Veronica's eyes shone. "I'm sure they find something to do with their time Taylor," Rebecca said. "I wouldn't worry about that. But how did you actually decide to get so involved with your spirituality?"

I signaled the waitress for more coffee and she freshened our cups. "Fifteen years ago, when I went back to school, I interned in the field of chemical dependency and learned about God as a higher power. This cracked the door between atheism and agnosticism wider. Then I read *A Course in Miracles*. If someone had told me five years before that I'd study a Christian based course, I would have told 'em they were nuts! But that's what I did. I read the material—every single day. I ignored the 'God' word at first. . . too many negative connotations for the feminist in me. Today, I like to say Goddess, All That Is, Universe or Love. Today, God and I get along much better."

"Talk about a complete turn around," Veronica said. "But what exactly is *A Course in Miracles*?"

"Yeah." Rebecca said. "What is it?"

Talk about religion and everyone gets all worked up. We were no exception. They leaned towards me. "It's a text and daily lessons that give you practice in changing your thinking from fear-based to love-based," I told them.

"Uh, huh. That sounds easy," Rebecca whispered sarcastically in Veronica's direction.

"Even though I lost it when I stepped off that cliff, I've had times when fear transformed to love. Listen to this. A couple years ago, I was visiting friends and ended up alone in the car with the one person who always makes my stomach knot up. One of the daily practices from the *Course* came to mind and I almost blew it off. With an—I'll believe it when I see it—attitude, I repeated 'I will forgive and this will disappear' a few times to myself and minutes later, we were laughing, my stomach was calm and I couldn't remember what made me uncomfortable in the first place. It sure felt like a miracle!"

"Anything else ladies?" Our waitress asked, sweeping the plates off the table.

"Just the check," Veronica said, digging into her purse.

Rebecca leaned toward me. "Don't you think if there really was only one way to do religion, someone would have found it by now? It makes me crazy the way some religions try to make us conform." She pulled her wallet out of her purse and threw a ten on the table.

"You're right," Veronica said. "Look at us. Donna chooses not to practice any religion at all, but like me, she loves nature and animals and children and that's spiritual—at least I think so. Linda is very in touch with spirit, but she doesn't go to church either. Gloria goes to Unity Church, which is non-denominational. Who's to say what's right and what's wrong?" Rebecca and I sat quietly. It was rare for Veronica to discuss the group. She's very private. "I love the way we always end our group with a meditation," she continued. "Sometimes, I'm so tired after work, I don't want to go, but then I do and I'm always glad. It's peaceful."

Our eyes met and I nodded. My mouth opened so wide in a yawn, I hurt my jaws. "If we don't stop now, we never will and I have to get up early tomorrow." We all scooted out of the booth, hugged and headed home.

At home, propped up in bed with pillows behind me, my electric heater warming my feet and my journal open, I drifted once again to thoughts of our group and the changes we were going through.

Suddenly a black, furry body hurtled herself into my lap, "Damn it Zurk! You know you're not allowed into the bedroom." I have two cats. I'm allergic to cats, and the compromise I've made to give myself some relief is to not allow them into the bedroom. After prying Zurk's nails out of my blanket, I heaved her out the door and shut it firmly. I settled myself back into bed and opened my journal. I have been spilling myself out onto the pages of journals since I was thirteen years old. My journal is my friend. There when I need to be listened to. Never disagrees with me. Unconditional, I suppose.

Change makes me feel upside down like the floor has shifted and tossed me into the air. Not just the major things like somebody dying, but even the smaller stuff, like a last minute change of plans, a plane being delayed or a trip postponed. I never know if I'll land on my head or my feet. Sometimes I think I have a choice, but usually how I land seems to be entirely decided by fate. Being out of control—that's what really scares me.

Fear's been with me my whole life. The chaos of mom and dad's alcoholism clenched my stomach most of my childhood. I'm tired of being controlled by fear. That's why I jumped off that cliff. To break through the fear I'd dragged with me. My newfound spirituality was trying to guide me to live differently. I didn't know how yet, but just like I knew I'd leap off that cliff, I knew I'd keep following the trail of love and joy.

I shut my journal and set it on the table. I curled up, hugging my pillow instead of my husband, Jim, who was out hang gliding with the boys.

Chapter 2

I woke up obsessing about the retreat, but I had too many clients to do anything about it until later that afternoon when I got on the phone. Linda had another obligation she just couldn't get out of. Rebecca wanted to go, but didn't know if she could get the time off work. Donna just laughed. "Why in the world would I want to go someplace where I'm gonna get whacko spirituality forced down my throat for an entire week?" Veronica had agreed to go at the meeting, but now she was having serious doubts. Gloria was the only one to commit to actually coming with me. Oh well, one traveling partner was better than none.

Two days later, Rebecca called and wanted to meet for lunch. Turn down food? No way. I met her at a place close to the gym where I work out. We've both lived in Lindston for over fifteen years, and it's such a relief to see it finally getting some happening eating spots. I'm from Long Beach, in Southern California, where pretty much anything goes, and Rebecca's home town is Sacramento, the state capital, so it was culture shock for both of us when we moved here. The Central Valley is conservative in general and Lindston is particularly so. It's my home now and I'm used to it, but I still miss the laid back, welcoming attitude of the beach crowd.

The Brighter Side was packed. Done up in art deco, it's a hole-in-the-wall place with excellent food and quick service. I grabbed a table and Rebecca came flying in a few minutes later. "Hey, Taylor!" she said waving.

"Hi! I can't believe how popular this place is." I handed her a menu.

"Seems like we always meet over food, huh?" she said, tossing her bag and coat into the booth.

"Yeah, but great food."

"God, I'm so glad you're not on a diet anymore." She looked at me with a question in her eyes. "You don't still worry about your weight, do you?"

I shrugged and set the menu down. "Not so much anymore. I'm in charge most of the time now." I've battled my weight since high school, and even though I make jokes about food and my weight, it is kind of a sore subject for me. I'm five feet six and small boned, and when I gain weight it shows immediately in my face and hips.

"Is that what they taught you in Overeaters Anonymous?"

I motioned for the waitress, over a sip of water. "I was really into meetings for a while. They helped me a lot and I had a great sponsor, but after a couple of years, I felt trapped by the structure and had to see if I could manage food on my own."

"Looks like you're doing great. You're not heavy at all," Rebecca said. She turned to the waitress and ordered a tuna on rye with potato salad. I ordered a small Cobb, dressing on the side.

"No, but I still carry about ten extra pounds. I'm not so hard on myself anymore, but I still have to watch obsessing about food But what woman doesn't? Seems like every woman I know fights herself over her weight or the thickness of her thighs. We're never totally satisfied."

Rebecca dumped a packet of Equal into her iced tea and took a long drink. She pushed her hair behind her ear. "Well, then no more talk about weight. Let me tell you about the dream I had. It was about this retreat too." She drained her glass. "O.K., I'm on a ship in the middle of the ocean. I can't see land. There are women from all over the world on the ship with me. I can tell there's an important event about to happen. The women are excited—the air feels electric. Just before the event starts, my beeper goes off. It's my husband. He tells me there's a client having an emergency and I have to go. I woke up—mad."

Rebecca and I are good therapists and we love to analyze our dreams. It's very true that we therapists like to take things apart. "Why do you think you were so mad?" I asked.

"Because it's the same old thing! Every time I want to do something for myself, something else always comes first—and I'm tired of it." Rebecca was rubbing her forehead so hard, red streaks were starting to appear.

"You know Rob would support you if you really wanted to go," I reminded her gently. "And your clients could certainly be without you for a week—mine are gonna have to."

She nodded. "I know he would." She pushed bits of tuna around on the plate, "I'm going Taylor. I don't know why, but I absolutely have to go."

I grabbed her arm and squeezed. "I'm so glad. It's going to be great."

Now there were three of us, Rebecca, Gloria and myself.

After a busy afternoon, I came home to a stack of messages—phone calls I had to return, appointments that had to be made or rescheduled. I left them on the counter by the phone and headed for the kitchen. Garlic, olive oil and Jim's baritone greeted me with a background chorus of cupboards opening and shutting. He gave me a noisy kiss, then turned back to the stove. Jim's gradually taken over most of the cooking. He's much better at it than I am anyway. After twenty years together, we have managed to find a nice balance between our routines. He just retired from his own small business and is now working hard at playing for a couple years, while I pay the bills. That was our agreement when he put me through school.

Besides cooking, Jim's passion is hang gliding. He spends most of his time with his flying buddies, jumping off cliffs. He's broken a bone here and there, but nothing major. I join them once in awhile, just to watch, not to fly, but I think it's good for him to have something of his own. He even entered the Nationals last year in his age group and placed in the top ten. He's my best friend. I like to think I'm his.

Over a delicious shrimp scampi, we talked about the retreat. As usual, Jim's enthusiasm for my "women's stuff" spilled over. I think he likes me going away on weekends once in a while, just so he can spend more time hang gliding. I sipped my wine, and looked across the table at my husband. Jim's one of the lucky guys. He just gets more attractive as he gets older. He's only fifty-two, but has the energy and sparkle of a thirty year old. I'm forty-five, and I have to struggle to keep up with him. He works out and keeps himself fit and firm and his wonderful, dark brown hair is so wild and curly that even a rubber band can hardly contain it—quite a contrast to my straight, white-blonde head of hair. And his humor is just like his hair—wild. He still makes me laugh. I guess that's why I never get tired of him.

"It'll be something if Donna goes," he said. "She thinks you girls are full of crap. I'll bet even you can't get her to go."

"You're on, buddy," I patted him on the hand. "How much?"

"Dinner," he said, holding up his glass. "Anywhere the winner chooses." We clinked glasses to seal the deal.

Jim loves to eat as much as I do, and we're always having bets revolving around food. He's a few pounds overweight also, but it just doesn't bother men like it does women. He certainly doesn't have a problem with it. Then again, he thinks I'm perfect just as I am.

Jim was picking up dishes and carrying them to the sink. "You've been to plenty of these retreats before,

29

Taylor, and I still don't quite understand why you like them so much."

I sipped my wine as I thought about it. Why do I like them so much? "I think for one thing, it's a special place where women can get away from the ordinary busy routines of their lives and take care of themselves. Time away allows us to find out who we are, especially women who are always taking care of others. In spiritual retreats we find out, sometimes for the first time, what a joy it is to be in a community with members of the same sex. It's fascinating to see the different personalities melding. Everyone comes with her own private thoughts and anxieties, excited and nervous, and wondering why they came in the first place."

I drained my glass and carried it to the sink, where Jim took it from me and carefully placed it in the dishwasher. "The best part is watching the women sharing and laughing together. It's so different for most of them to be waited on at first, but by the last day, they're getting used to it. By the time we leave, it feels like we've been friends forever. I think it changes our understanding about women as friends."

Jim closed the dishwasher and pushed the ON button. It shuddered into action. "Sounds like fun. What about men and women together?"

I shook my head. "It's taken me a while to get to this place, but at least for now, I think it's better to keep things separate. When we're in mixed groups, the women tend to subjugate themselves and I'm sure men act differently too. Not good or bad, just different."

Jim and I sat back down at the table. "I did read 'Men are From Mars. . . ', ya know, so I kind of get what you mean. Still, I feel left out." He reached over and ran his fingers along my jaw. "But. . . even if I do feel left out, I still want you to go off with your friends and howl at the moon or whatever you do." He grinned at me.

"Is that what you think we do—howl at the moon?"

"Well, I know you've done it at least once." He was running his fingers lightly down the inside of my arm. Drives me wild.

"Yeah, and it was fun to let the wild woman out." On Jim's lap now, I hugged him and gave him a long, slow kiss. We turned out the lights and went to bed.

Chapter 3

Later that week I kept thinking about the retreat and how to inspire the others to join us. I like to let people make their own decisions, so I was slightly uncomfortable thinking I should try to persuade them to go. But again, that strong pull in my gut was trying to direct me and I felt compelled to listen.

Getting ready for work, phone calls and animals attempting to divert my attention, I had a blaze of inspiration. "Linda. . . Hi. I know, things are crazy here too. Listen can you squeeze me in for a massage today? Four-fifteen, great. I'll be there." I put the phone down. Well, even if it didn't work, I really could use a massage.

Stretched out face down on the padded table, after a frantic day, Linda's expert fingers worked their magic. My shoulders relaxed and I lay quiet, enjoying the attention. "Have you decided anything yet Linda, about the retreat?" Casual, that's me.

"Sometimes I just feel overwhelmed," she said as she rolled her knuckles into my shoulder. Yeow! "I have a deep sense this retreat is going to be life-changing and I don't know if I'm ready for another major change right now. Sometimes I think that things are happening so fast I can barely keep up. I guess I just feel scared." I mumbled my understanding, enjoying the total relaxation of my body.

Linda's strong hands kneaded my back as if it was bread dough that she was hoping would rise. "Learning about my spirituality has been great," she said, ". . . for the most part anyway. But I keep remembering what one of my teachers told me. He said that as we get in touch with our inner selves, our old emotional baggage comes up and it has to be dealt with. That's been true for me so far and it's not fun."

"Yeah, but sometimes things that aren't fun can be really great for us. We both know that underneath the layers of human needs and personality is the essence of who we really are—unconditional love. Enlightenment is like peeling an onion, revealing layer after layer of ourselves until we find our true nature. But, I know how you feel," I acknowledged, trying to reassure her as I rolled over and sat up. "We've all been through a lot of ups and downs over the last two years. It's up to you, and believe me, if you decide not to go I'll understand."

All of a sudden I felt released from trying to convince her and reconnected with a trust that whether she attended or not it was O.K.. I left Linda and my massage physically relaxed, and mentally calm.

That evening I called Veronica. Like every doctor I know, she can only be found at home evenings and occasional weekends. Her schedule is crammed with patients; I don't know how she does it. Sometimes, she admits, she doesn't either. She's opened my eyes to what physicians go through, from grueling medical school to the grinding daily routines of trying to accommodate patients' needs with Managed Care. I don't envy her workload. Doctors have prestige, but I wonder if the demands of the job are a fair trade.

Finally I got her on the phone. She'd been non-committal about the retreat after our evening at the cafe, but she was usually game to attend anything that sounded interesting. We talked for a while, catching up on what books we were reading. She's the only person I know who reads more than I do. When I asked her if she'd made a decision about the retreat, she sounded defeated. "I want to go, you know me, I love my weekends off and being in the mountains, but I've been off quite a bit recently. I just don't know if I can get the time away. I'll know within a couple weeks, then I'll get back to you."

I told her Gloria was fully committed and Rebecca had stated her intention, not yet sure how she'd make it happen. We agreed to check in with each other again soon.

In bed that night, I worked on my journal. I questioned some of my thoughts about life, the spiritual journey and what it means.

Is destiny just a mumbo jumbo word that New Agers manipulate to give themselves permission to act the way their ego wants? Or is there really another dimension, an unseen world, where we can receive guidance, answers, and comfort? I wrote on. *I know there's a growing group of people from all over the world, that are turning inward toward the LIGHT of their Higher Self or more true nature. They're searching for answers in balance with seeking guidance from outside resources such as family, friends, church, counselor or God. Spirituality may be expressed in particular traditional forms such as Christianity, Judaism or Buddhism, but the driving force and common theme behind it is LOVE.*

One thing I know is that my life has changed for the better since I've learned to pay attention to my inner feelings, my dreams and inner imagery. My gut feelings are as important to my life as the time and energy I spend working, being with people I care about and dealing with the daily details of life.

This heavy thinking was putting me to sleep. I opened the window inviting in the warm night air of summer, turned off my light and fell instantly asleep.

At work the next day I had an inspiration about how to get the rest of the group to the retreat. (So much for allowing and letting go.) My inspired plan was to invite a friend of mine to "channel" for the group. Marie is not a member of our group, but she knows most of us. She began "channeling" about a year ago and I thought it'd be fun to hear what she has to say.

I first heard about channeling from a long-term, and quite sane, friend of mine, Toni. Before that I thought channeling must be only for the most radical New Ager. Toni's first experience with channeling came after reading a Shirley MacLaine book. She went into meditation and was instructed by a voice inside to turn on her tape recorder, which she very skeptically did. At the end of the meditation she couldn't remember much and rewound the tape and played what turned out to be channeled material about her higher nature and what would be happening over the next few years. She thought it was interesting, didn't take it too seriously, but continued to listen to the voice inside and occasionally record it.

It's been ten years since Toni invited me for a visit that changed my perception of reality.

It was a gorgeous spring day when I crossed the Dumbarton Bridge into Palo Alto. Wind whipped the water into white caps. I had my windows down and the pungent sea air made my nose tingle. I've always loved going to the Bay Area, but especially then because I was guaranteed an interesting lunch or dinner as we always went somewhere wonderful to eat. As I turned into Toni's driveway I honked my horn. Grabbing my new overnight bag and books out of my old Ford Galaxy 500, I headed up her front steps.

"Taylor!" She grabbed my bag. "Come in. God, it's so good to see you!" She dropped the bag on the couch and gave me a warm hug. Toni and I have been friends as long as I can remember. She's got just as much energy as I do and absolutely loves to laugh, which she does often and loudly. We always have fun together.

After barely getting settled, she flashed me a warm smile. "Taylor, you've gotta meet Mauve."

"Mauve?"

She nodded, brown eyes on fire. "He's the old guy that channels through me. You know, I told you about it a couple months ago. You want to see if he'll come today?"

I vaguely remembered her mentioning her channeling experience. "Well, uh, I don't know exactly what you mean, but I'm game. What do we do?"

She pointed to the middle of the living room floor and suggested we sit on the pillows she had already placed there. She turned on the tape recorder and settled herself on a pillow. "Just relax and watch me. I'm never sure he'll come, but let's try." She closed her eyes and started breathing deeply.

I didn't say anything, but I felt weird inside. My stomach was jumping around, and my hands were damp. What was I doing here?

"I need to say a prayer of protection to make sure that only positive loving energy comes through," Toni said, settling deeper into the cushion. "I close my aura to all except the light of my 'I AM' presence. I affirm and confirm that only energy that is for the highest good come through now."

I sat in complete silence. Then Toni's body started gently rocking back and forth. All of a sudden I felt an energetic shift in the room and a man's voice emanated from her. I held my breath. The voice was much deeper than Toni's but squeaky and her body had taken on a very different posture. She was hunched over with one arm up, and appeared to be puffing on something. Her mouth was skewed to one side and it looked like she didn't have any teeth.

I couldn't believe what I was seeing. I had a million questions, but I couldn't move, much less speak. I drifted off for a moment. My perception of the person in front of me felt upside down. Was I being tricked? Toni appeared so different, not just how she looked, but how it felt to be with her.

"Yes, I am Mauve. Is there something I can do for you?" he asked.

Mauve's question brought me back to the moment. "I'm feeling strange about talking to someone who is here, but not here," I said. "I'd like to know more about you first. Who are you, why are you here and where do you come from?"

"I am Mauve. I am a guide and friend of Toni's. I've been with her over many lifetimes, the most recent was in the Southwest where I was like a grandfather to her. I've come to give her some assistance with her spiritual journey as agreed to before she came into this lifetime." Mauve was smacking his lips, holding his arm up towards his mouth.

This isn't Toni, I remember thinking. I ceased thinking about this body in front of me as only Toni's because the personality coming through, the body posture and the voice were creating a clear sense of a unique being.

"Are you smoking a pipe?" I suddenly realized what the arm posture and smacking probably were.

"Yes, one of the habits I miss most about my last physical life," chuckled Mauve rocking back and forth.

"And it looks like you're rocking."

"I am. I used to love to sit on my porch and look out over the desert and smoke my pipe in the years after I couldn't work my ranch. I had a little place just out of town and would sit for hours rocking. Little Martha, as she was called then, would come and talk to me and tell her troubles and I listened and gave her comfort and rocked her in my lap. She was a beautiful little girl and grew into a beautiful young woman. In that lifetime, as in this one, she didn't have a supportive family and she felt different from others. I helped her to not feel so alone. Any questions you would like help with, dear?"

"I don't know how to do this and I feel a little scared talking to someone I don't know. This is weird, Mauve."

He chuckled again from deep in his throat and continued to puff on his invisible pipe.

"I'm here and will wait until you're ready."

"Can I ask questions about other people in my life?"

"Yes, within limit, as I won't reveal anything that would be harmful to another."

I asked him questions about my relationship with my husband and son. I found out that the three of us had been together in many lifetimes and that was why we felt so close in this one. I learned to trust his integrity. I asked about my sister-in-law about whom I had some misgivings. He refused to answer because he didn't know whether or not I might misuse the information.

"It's time to end this talk as Toni's body is getting tired. I have enjoyed our talk and I hope I'll see you again." With that he was quiet for a few moments and slowly Toni's body shook off his posture and hers asserted itself. She stretched and yawned and opened her eyes.

"Oh, I'm so stiff. What happened?" she asked.

"Don't you remember anything?"

"Not much. I feel like I'm way far away when Mauve comes through and sometimes I can hear him, but I can't really remember afterwards. Why does my jaw hurt?" she asked rubbing her face.

I described how Mauve holds her body while coming through her and about his pipe smoking and rocking.

"It was scary Toni, but exciting too when his energy came into the room and your body started changing posture."

We talked about the information Mauve gave me and didn't give me, which actually made me trust him more. I felt like any questions I asked would be sifted through, respected but not answered if any harm could come to me or someone else.

Over the next three or four years I had an opportunity to speak with Mauve many times and we became friends. Weird to say that a non-bodied personality temporarily coming through my friend could feel like a friend, but he did. When he told Toni he was moving on, I think I missed him more than she did because of the many fun, witty, thought-provoking conversations I had with him.

We videotaped him one time so she could see how she appeared while doing what I now know is called "full-body channeling." She was amazed at the contortions her body went through to allow Mauve to smoke his pipe while rocking in his chair and appearing to be toothless.

It was important to Toni that every time she was preparing to channel she offered a prayer of protection so that only loving energy would come through and only information that was for the highest good. I used to think there were no negative or evil energies in the unseen world, but now I know that's not true. After working with clients that have been satanically, ritualistically abused and listening to their horror stories, I *know* there are dark forces.

The one time Toni forgot to do her protection prayer a dark and heavy energy force started to enter. The room felt awful, and I felt like I was suffocating. I yelled at Toni to come out of her trance. It took a few seconds of my yelling and then grabbing her before she was able to wake up. She thanked me for bringing her back because it was a negative energy which had been trying to take over. Later, when Mauve came through he said it was really good we were able to bring Toni back because that had truly been a negative spirit which might have used Toni's body as a vehicle and harmed me. He didn't go into more detail and neither one of us wanted to know more about what could have happened.

Toni and I had many conversations about our experiences with Mauve, questioning and analyzing what channeling really is. There are different theories and there are different kinds of channeling. In full-body channeling, the Being or personality comes through and sounds and looks different than the original person. Then there's a softer type, where information comes through in the individual's own voice, with no body changes. There are channels who are fully conscious while the energy is coming through and others, like Toni, who aren't.

Many of us receive information in the form of inspiration during meditation or we lapse into a trance-like state, for example, while driving. At other quiet times one gets a particular image or thought that feels important to jot down or notice. Really, channeling isn't any big deal. All of us have the ability to open ourselves to a higher aspect of consciousness. If it's true that everything in the Universe is connected, or is ONE, then anyone or thing that comes through is a part of that Oneness, or God energy. Even the dark energy is part of the Oneness.

Through channeling and other experiences, I've learned to become what Betty Bethards, author of *The Dream Book*, calls an "open-minded skeptic." I take in what fits and explore the new possibilities without automatically rejecting something because it doesn't agree with my known beliefs and attitudes. I take much of what the so-called New Age has to offer in the spirit of fun. I've played with tarot cards and gone to psychics and healers over the last few years. Like a child being introduced to new toys that are fun and educational, many of these tools have helped me to stretch beyond my limited thinking, over-analytical mind to the greater possibility and wholeness of who I am.

Toni doesn't like to channel in front of groups, so it was Marie I decided to call to channel for our women's group. She is an angel of a woman. Light and love emanate from her and she's one of those people you always feel good around. She draws people out of themselves and she has fun bringing her own brand of spirituality into her workplace. Marie really is good.

I got her on the phone at her office. "Hi! Long time no see. How'd you like to come to our next women's meeting and channel?" I had told her about the retreat and while she wasn't able to make it, she thought it sounded wonderful.

She laughed, "Sure, I'm game. But, I have no idea what the guide will say. It could backfire on you. Spirit doesn't usually tell people what to do, so I don't know if I'll help convince the others to go, but, it'd be fun to see what might come through. What's the day and time?"

Well, I thought, as I hung up the phone, this'll either get them more interested, or turn them off completely. I'm sure Donna will have a few choice things to say. I hurried out the door and home to Jim's vegetable lasagna.

Chapter 4

The month blazed by and the next women's meeting was at my house. Jim and I have lived in this same suburban neighborhood for about fifteen years. He and our son, Rich, both attended Fremont Elementary School and had the same shop teacher 25 years apart. I found the continuity strange because the longest I had ever lived in one place as a child was eight years.

Our home is decorated in a Southwestern style and we've picked up different art work and knick knacks from our various trips to Santa Fe and Phoenix over the years. It's a comfortable home and people feel nurtured here. Windows across the back of the house open out to a lush green backyard. We have a hammock swinging between two large trees and one of the after work de-stressors we enjoy in the warm months is having dinner on the back patio, then lying in the hammock discussing the day and weekly activities with each other. Squeezed up tight next to Jim in that hammock, sharing our thoughts, is the most relaxing place on earth.

Seven o'clock Thursday night, the girls started to arrive. Rebecca, Veronica and Gloria came tumbling in, laughing and talking. By the time Donna and then Linda joined us, the house was humming with energy. Everyone was excited—even Donna, though she made it clear she didn't believe in "other worldly people," as she put it. Marie was nervous. She didn't do group channelings very often and channeling was still fairly new for her. After everyone settled down with drinks, cookies or both, and we had a chance to catch up on the basics of what was going on in each of our lives, we turned the meeting over to Marie.

She smiled beautifully and asked us to meditate with her for a few minutes to prepare the room so that we would all harmonize our energies together. We quieted ourselves. I began to focus on my breath as it seems to be the only thing that helps my busy mind unwind.

Marie offered a prayer of protection: "Spirit, let this channeling be for the highest good and only for the highest good. Let me be a clear channel for the perfect information to come through now that is of the highest guidance for this group. So be it." We all waited silently and expectantly with our eyes closed. And patiently. Well, most of us waited patiently. I'm still working on that one.

In Marie's voice, but a bit deeper and more full, came the following words: "Greetings. We are so pleased to be called to offer guidance to you. We are grateful for your coming together as this is a time of great importance in your world. Important for earth, and for the whole

Universe. As those of you who are working with the LIGHT and increasing your loving vibrations continue to heal the unhealed places within, expand your ability to love yourselves, feel compassionate toward all, then by your presence, in whatever job or situation you're in, whether teacher, office worker, politician, etc., you are building the scope of love, and helping others to open to their higher selves.

"The retreat is one opportunity to learn more about yourselves and be in community with other women. Anytime you can give yourselves permission to be away from the stress and strain of daily work and allow more quiet time is worthwhile. Inner work is as important as outer work. Your world has been out of balance with the demands of work, home, family and friends, taking precedence over time spent focusing within. Any time spent learning, expanding and quieting your thinking, thinking, thinking, 'monkey minds' is worthwhile.

"You must go within and discover for yourselves if this particular retreat is the one you wish to attend. We ask you to do that now for a few minutes and see what your own answers are. Thank-you. That is all."

We spent the next twenty minutes in silence with our own thoughts and breath. Without anyone saying anything we all came out of meditation at about the same time, stretching and opening our eyes. One by one the group members shared their experience of the channeling and quiet time.

Donna, not being a meditator, but respectful of the rest of us, shared first. "You know I think this channeling stuff is weird. But the one thing I liked about what you said Marie is that we all need to come up with our own answers. We need to figure out for ourselves whether attending this retreat is what we want to do. Whether it's 'spirit' or just you talking, I appreciate that there's never any judgement, just an openness and a sense that we'll decide for ourselves in the way that's best for us. I still don't know if I'm going to go or not, but the one reason I would go is just to hang out with all of you for a few days because we always have such fun together."

I became more deeply aware during my meditation of the need to not orchestrate and to let go of trying to control whether others would attend the retreat or not.

I stood up and stretched. "If you know you're going, leave your check or visa number tonight and I'll make sure your reservation is handled. Oh, and I just want to let you all know that even though I hope you come—you *know* we'll have fun—don't feel pressured, O.K.?" Donna rolled her eyes and Gloria burst out laughing.

"But," I continued, grinning, "the retreat's only a month away!"

We finished our meeting with our traditional meditation and healing circle, set the time for our next meeting and walked outside to admire the new cars three of us had recently purchased. I bought a new Camaro a couple months ago, Rebecca a new Jaguar and Gloria a new Saturn. We were all delighted talking about the advantages of our cars, the options, and for me, a sports car was such an extravagant gesture. My old car was a perfectly great Toyota Corolla—boring but functional, and I loved it. But, it sure is different to get in my new car. I feel special.

"Girlfriends, you know what I find interesting about driving this car?" I asked. Gloria and Rebecca stopped talking. "I get more guys waving at me and trying to talk to me. It pisses me off. It's not me, it's the car." I shook my head.

"I disagree," Gloria said. "I look more at guys in great cars. I think the car allows them to see you. After all, blonde, cute, why wouldn't they look?" She laughed and Veronica and Linda nodded.

"I'm still feeling embarrassed about my new car," Rebecca said. "I squirm every time a client sees me in this Jaguar. I want to explain that I got it because my aunt left it to me in her will. But, I love it. I just have to be careful about the tickets—it's easy to go eighty and not feel it." Rebecca made a face and fiddled around with her car control keys to find the right button to push to open the doors.

"That's one of the things I love about you, Rebecca, so unassuming about being a rich bbb. . . " She looked at me with her eyebrow up as I finished. ". . . woman." *Whew, where did that come from?* I laughed, shaky. I knew exactly where it had come from. When Rebecca drove up in her new Jag, I was jealous. I didn't share my feelings with her because I knew she was uncomfortable enough. Switching gears I asked her. "Have you sold your Datsun yet?"

"No, but I know it'll sell. There must be another forty plus year old woman out there who's having a mid-life crisis and needs a sports car."

"Isn't that the truth! Besides myself, I bet I know three women who have bought sports cars recently. It must be a female fortyish-rite-of-passage," I laughed.

We hugged and talked about our next get-together. When they got into their cars and left, I waved goodbye and walked back into the house. Jim got home within a few minutes and I shared our conversation about forty plus women buying sports cars. He laughed and told me again how happy he was I had bought the car I wanted.

As I climbed into bed that evening I felt so blessed to have my women friends and to know they felt the same about me. Every month I look forward to our group, anticipating our time together. I always learn something. The high energy we all experience usually lasts a couple days after the meeting and I always sleep wonderfully the night of the group. For someone who has trouble sleeping that's a grateful event.

Chapter 5

Twice a week, sometimes three times, Linda joins me for my morning walk-jog. She only lives a mile or so away, but between her job and her kids, finding the time is a stretch. She fell into step with me as my golden retriever, Annie, darted back and forth. We walked in silence for a couple minutes, enjoying the crisp October air. My street, Cherrywood, is in an older part of Lindston. Lined with large, airy ash trees, it's quiet—serene—especially at six-fifteen in the morning.

"Have I mentioned my workshops to you?"

Linda shook her head. "I don't think so—go ahead, what are they?"

"My workshops are called 'Embracing Change'. I use Movement Awareness and imagery as the teaching instruments. One reason I'm so curious about this retreat is because I want to see how someone else teaches change."

We picked up the pace a little, pumping our arms in rhythm. I continued. "Movement Awareness is a body-oriented psychotherapy. I learned about it in graduate school. It uses postures and movements to help you become more aware of who you really are. We Westerners are so good at thinking and not so comfortable with our body as a learning tool, but I know that body movements teach us as much about ourselves as our thinking mind. Being a massage therapist, Linda, you understand how body movements can teach us more about ourselves than our thinking mind."

Linda's curls bobbed up and down in agreement. "I know exactly. When I was first getting massages during massage school I couldn't believe all the emotions I felt as different parts of my body were worked on. I had anger trapped in my shoulders and back. Images would come up of being a child, for example, or a fight I had with my mom. I guess I stuffed some of those feelings into my shoulders." She stooped to pick up Annie's ball and throw it for her, wiping her hand afterwards on the dog slobber rag I handed her, that I always take on my walks.

"Do you know what I found to be *the* thing we adults are most uncomfortable with? Change, and the older we get the harder it is."

We were about half-way through our walk. Our usual route is partly through alleys so I can have Annie off the leash and wear her out chasing her ball. Then we like to hit the college district of our town. The homes are uniquely designed and we never tire of admiring them.

Linda nodded thoughtfully as she increased the pumping of her arms. "Young kids are just who they are," she said. "They don't worry about what anyone else thinks. They're really in the present moment, aren't they? But, that changes as kids get older. I wish there was a way to keep part of ourselves as much in the moment as we are when we're little." Linda kicked our pace up to a slow jog and I fell in step with her—our tennis shoes slapping the pavement noisily.

Annie came flying over to me, her tail an orange flag, as she dropped her gooey lump of a ball at my feet. Linda and I both laughed as we watched her obvious glee—she couldn't wait for me to throw her lump. "See," I said as I heaved it. "Annie's thrilled just to have me right here, right now, throwing her ball for her." We watched her tear after it and grab it in her mouth. She was wagging her tail proudly as she trotted back and joined us.

A half-mile later, I was huffing and puffing as we slowed to a walk to catch our breath. "I don't think children get in their own way by over-analyzing the changes they go through," I said, holding my side. "A child doesn't sit around and think about why it's time for them to go from crawling to walking, they just *do it*. We adults scare ourselves or stop ourselves by the 'what-if' games we play. Children are in the flow of life. Just going along without leaking or losing energy. I think children and animals are alike. They're both in touch with their being natures. They haven't learned to protect themselves from life by thinking and doing.

"Seems like children have a lot to teach us about how to embrace change instead of avoiding it. They are so used to the ground beneath them seeming to be liquid. Everything is changing. Their size, ability to move, understand, talk and think. And it's so exciting! The world is a curious and wonderful place for them."

"Children that aren't abused or neglected, you mean," Linda said.

"Well sure. They have to spend too much energy just surviving." We walked in silence. I hate the thought of little kids being abused—makes me crazy. I tried to shrug it off.

"But, still, think about the child. Everything is new or unknown. We're born not knowing, yet the scariest thing about change is the *unknown*. I wonder how we learn to fear the unknown when we used to take it for granted and were O.K. with it?

"One more thing and then I'll shut up about change. I just read that Sigmund Freud, who I bear no great love for, said that we're born with only two fears; the fear of falling and the fear of loud noises."

Linda's eyebrows shot up. "God, that means we learn the rest. . . yuk! Hey, we're almost back to the house. I can't believe it. Seems like we just left. Thanks for the wonderful walk and conversation."

Linda and I said our goodbyes as she got into her car and set off for the typical busy day of professional woman, mother and wife. I put Annie in the backyard panting and heading for her water bowl as I went into the house to get ready for my workday.

I saw a number of clients in the morning and then got ready for a luncheon appointment with Gloria. At least one of my encounters with friends today hadn't included food; the food addict part of me still feels guilty at times for planning get-togethers around eating, as if I'm not supposed to find eating pleasurable. Gloria loves to eat as much as the rest of us so we met and I filled her in on our conversation this morning.

Gloria told me she recently saw *The Bridges of Madison County* and described the scene where Robert Kincaid, the photographer, attempts to explain to his Iowa housewife lover, Francesca, that change can be as comforting as finding safety in the familiar. Francesca fights this concept because it's so different from what she's experienced in her farm family existence, where she found a niche that was safe but also stultifying at times. For Francesca, leaving the familiar for the freedom Robert Kincaid asked of her was to stretch herself beyond the limits she felt capable of risking.

"What Robert Kincaid asked of Francesca was too much of a leap and it reminds me of when I left the business world, went back to school and totally changed my career," Gloria said, licking her fingers. The complimentary chips were divine. "Remember how scared I was? It was awful. I felt like I was on a cliff about to leap and leaving behind the security of that wonderful paycheck every week. I didn't think Gary could handle making the leap with me. He wanted to cling to familiar ground. Remember when he told me that he expected me to stay the same as when we married? He married a professional business woman and that's how he wanted me to stay. I'm so grateful I had my friends who encouraged me. I couldn't have done it without all your support." Gloria was smiling at me as she continued.

"What I've gotten for taking that leap has been worth it, I may not have a steady dependable income but I feel ALIVE and I love what I do. I love helping other people get in shape and feel good physically. It's so much fun. It's worth the moments of insecurity and dread that come up sometimes around the first of the month when the rent's due. It was the perfect choice for me."

We ordered a Caesar salad and a vegetarian burger and split it like we often do so we can have dessert—also split. We were at Randino's, a cafe with an outside seating area with beautiful greenery and lots of shade.

"When I took your class it came at a great time for me," Gloria said. "I was struggling with leaving a $60,000 a year job and it helped me understand that the changes we go through have a beginning, a middle and an end. When I became aware that I was ending one career and needed to grieve those losses, and beginning a new career with the typical fears of beginnings, it helped me relax and feel more peaceful. 'Course, at the time, I was also moving and ending a marriage in which my husband didn't want me to change. I was on overload! I learned it wasn't me that was crazy but all the changes that made me feel like I was. Ah, our food."

The burger was great. As we ate, we talked about my relationship with Jim and just caught up in general. When we finished our lunch, I told Gloria how much I appreciated her boldness in doing what she felt she had to do to change her career and live her passion, despite not knowing when or how much money was coming in from month to month. "And, I really want you to come on this retreat. We've gotta find out what this great change is all about," I told her.

"You got that right," Gloria agreed.

We paid our bill, walked to our cars, gave each other a big hug and headed back to our respective afternoons.

That night I lay in bed listening to Jim's regular snores—something I've accepted over the years. I couldn't help wondering what exactly this great change could be? Is it just a spiritual change? Is it the changing of awareness from not trusting the unknown to trusting it? Hmm. . .

Chapter 6

As it turned out Veronica found a colleague to cover for her, Donna decided she didn't want to miss a week out in nature and with her friends, and even Linda was able to leave husband and children to fend for themselves. I wasn't at all surprised by circumstances ironing themselves out to launch us into this journey. One of my favorite books is *The Celestine Prophecy*. It talks about how important it is to notice events that seem like coincidences. Not to over-analyze, just notice and enjoy the mystery of life. I was determined to do just that.

On Monday I was thinking and planning what I wanted to have with me for the week. I tend to over-pack and so was arranging and rearranging my stuff. Of course, I had my books with me, in a separate bag. I also had snacks. Bananas and bagels, for those in-the-middle-of-the-night awakenings and I definitely had enough clothes to change every day, plus a couple of extra outfits so that I had a choice about what to wear. Everything fit perfectly into my extra large suitcase that Jim nicknamed "Big Bertha." I was ready!

Tuesday morning I got a call from Linda whose husband was having a tough time with her being gone for a week. "I don't know if I should go or not. I know this is silly, but a week feels like such a long time. I'm just not sure Ted and the kids can get along without me for a whole week. I think I'm feeling scared. I've never been gone that long without Ted and the kids, just myself with no responsibilities and no kids demanding my time. God, it seems so selfish!"

I tried to reassure her. "I know how you feel. The first time I went to a retreat, I was terrified. I went by myself so I was in totally new territory. But, you know, everyone felt the same way. Yuk, at that retreat everyone camped and you know me, I'm a Hilton Camper. Putting up my tent by myself was interesting! I felt like such an idiot. But, I did it. I drove down the dirt path that led out of the camp site a week later, so high with my expanded sense of Self and possibility, I decided any discomfort was well worth it. And, Linda, remember, this retreat is in a very nice home with beds."

"Well, I'm going, I'm not backing out," she said firmly, "but there is a part of me that would just like to be safe and comfy forever in my own little world and never have to venture out. Other parts keep pulling me forward to my true nature. I guess that's good. Thanks for listening, I feel better. Oh, I almost forgot, I've got the van, so I can drive."

We hung up after deciding we'd all meet at Linda's and load the van on Friday.

Seven-thirty Friday morning, the six of us parked our cars and ran into the house to go to the bathroom one last time before getting on the road. The retreat was about five hours away in the hills above Mendocino. We threw our bags in the back of the van—I won the "who has the most luggage contest"—and piled in to make ourselves comfy for the drive.

When I drive with passengers in the car I try to keep my eyes on the road while talking, but you know how some people feel the need to have eye contact with everyone they are talking with, no matter the terrain? About half-way through the last trip with Linda driving, I started deep breathing to calm my anxiety. She kept turning around and looking at the person in the back of the van. Drove me nuts! Then, there was the narrow miss of the turn-off with a swerving to avoid the freeway center divider. We survived. But I took time later to gently let her know how anxious I had been. She assured me at the start of this trip she now knew how I wanted her to drive. I said a silent prayer of affirmation for a safe, fun trip.

I love women, and traveling with a group of women friends I enjoy and appreciate is so much fun. There's such freedom, excitement, enthusiasm and passion. It's great. I've noticed that when women get together, we are more ourselves. I imagine it's the same for men. I love my husband Jim and we have a terrific time together, but the emotional closeness I share with him is very different from that of my women friends.

Driving with women can be hell, if you're not a woman. We like to stop. To pee, to eat, to sightsee, check the directions or just to stretch our legs. Before we set out we all looked at the map and made various comments and interpretations of what the notations appeared to mean. I'm a good map reader, but I'm also directionally challenged. However, I was sure that with six of us consulting we'd get there with no real problems and if we did have a detour or two, well, we had the car phone.

Traveling women talk non-stop. It's fun. Our five hour drive stretched to seven. When one or two of us needed a break from the interaction, we'd just pull out a book or close our eyes and nap. There's such acceptance with all of us that we allow each woman to do what she feels she needs to do to take care of herself.

We talked a lot about Mendocino's charms. Set on and above the ocean with many of the original buildings and homes of a hundred years ago intact, it's picture postcard pretty. There are wonderful restaurants and we vowed that after the retreat we'd stop at the Cafe Beaujolais where a couple of us had experienced dreamed about meals.

We followed our directions north of Mendocino and into the foothills. A well-maintained dirt road took us through beautiful trees and the air was awash in musky pine. The rich salty smell of ocean wafted into the car and I realized I was anxious.

"Anyone else nervous?" I asked the group. "My stomach is doing the rumba!"

"Are you kidding?" Rebecca said. "I've been sick for the last forty-five minutes! I thought it was just my Dramamine wearing off."

Everyone else, except Donna, agreed. She thought she wasn't going to get that much out of the retreat, and was just along to enjoy the fresh air, good food, and our company. "So how many other whacko women are going to be at this retreat?" she asked loudly.

"Good question. I'm sure there'll be others. I think the number of women that could attend was limited to ten. I love meeting new people!" Almost there, I was getting curious about who else would be at the retreat.

We started keeping an eye open for the retreat house. Few homes littered the foothills and all were different with interesting features. We saw a rustic cabin with peeling paint and an under-maintained yard, a stunning two story Cape Cod with immaculate everything, a home that looked like a converted farm house and finally, yes, 1032 Lotus Way, our retreat destination. Multicolored flowers lined the front of the driveway, and eucalyptus trees escorted our van through the entrance of the estate embracing and welcoming us with their wild aroma. I immediately calmed.

The house was two storied, right out of Architectural Digest. The sun had bleached the wood light blonde and lots of windows provided a view inside. A long lazy porch stretched across the front and wrapped around one side. Rocking and lounge chairs were scattered about haphazardly. Hanging plants and flowers in purples and blues, with a few white petunias for contrast, were strategically placed for color. We all oohed and aahed as we found a parking place and piled out of the van.

"We've hit the jackpot! This is wonderful, isn't it?" I said as I maneuvered my luggage out of the back of the van. The air, the beauty of the place, everything looked and felt right, safe and comfortable.

As the rest of the group got their stuff, a woman opened the side door of the house and walked onto the porch. Blonde, about 5'5", with long legs reaching forever from white shorts, she wore a white long-sleeved linen blouse pushed up her arms and a huge smile on her face as she gracefully strode forward to greet us.

"Oh, I'm so glad you're here. You must be the group from Lindston. We've been wondering when you'd get here. That road between Willits and Mendocino can be treacherous. My name is Tanya," she said in a smooth, cultured voice. "Why don't you follow me as soon as you have all your things."

Her blonde hair was held up in a pony tail with wisps trailing along the sides of her face. She looked young, late twenties, maybe early thirties, but she was purposeful and conveyed a confidence in herself.

We all introduced ourselves as we followed, filling her in on the trip and complimenting her on the house.

She smiled. "We feel blessed to have this home available to us for our retreats. It belongs to a wealthy friend of ours, a woman who has made her fortune in real estate and wants to give back to other women. She rents it to us every year two or three times for a very reasonable amount. She's helped us set up a scholarship fund to support women who come to our retreats who wouldn't otherwise be able to do so."

The house was large, 5,000 square feet. It had six bedrooms for guests and two for the teachers on the other side of the house. Each bedroom was decorated differently and the one Rebecca and I got was hued in soft pinks and complementary mauves. There were two full size four-poster beds covered in beautiful patchwork comforters of multicolored silk. Two antique rocking chairs upholstered in mauve with intricately carved wooden arms sat in opposing corners.

"I love these chairs," I said, dropping into one. "This style was made around the turn of the century for women to do their needle work. They're smaller than the rockers we have now and fit me perfectly." I pushed myself back and rocked quietly as Rebecca checked out the bathroom.

The French doors in our second story room opened onto a small deck that looked out over the back foothills. The clean smell of eucalyptus and pine greeted us as Rebecca flung wide the doors, "I'm so happy to be here I could cry," she said, filling her lungs. "And I feel so at home. . . Oh, life is good!"

"Yeah, girlfriend, did we luck out, or what? Which bed do you want?" She threw her luggage on the one away from the window and closest to the bathroom. Perfect, I could look down on the yard and over at the mountains from my bed.

Tanya had told us we had an hour or so to get settled in before hors d'oeuvres. Spurred on by our vivid imaginings of what culinary delights might be awaiting us, Rebecca and I organized our stuff in the dressers and armoires and staked out our cosmetic territories on the bathroom counters. And, what counter tops! A beautiful granite, sand color with bits of white and a darker sand for contrast and polished to a bright gleam. There was a huge Jacuzzi tub and a separate glassed-in shower. I love beautiful bathrooms—feels so decadent.

"Kind of like staying at the Ritz! I wonder if they have room service?" I laughed.

"What happened to talking about food?" Rebecca complained. "Food's a lot more fun than money!"

"I couldn't agree more." As we were leaving, I saw a multi-colored folder on the dresser by the door and glanced inside. It was an information packet with sheets of rose colored paper and an agenda for the week with instructions for an autobiography we were to complete by the fourth day of the retreat.

"Look at this" I murmured. "I wasn't expecting to write my life story. Wonder why?" Rebecca stood next to me, reading over my shoulder.

"There's one girlfriend who's definitely going to wake up or bail—Donna." Rebecca stretched out on the bed and continued to read her packet.

The general assignment was to chronologically put down the major details of our life from birth to present. Questions like how many in your family of origin, your birth order, how your birth order affected you in the family and in life since growing up. Who was the person who saw us for who we really were as a child. Was that helpful? Or, if we didn't have anyone, how we compensated or found those parts of ourselves.

We were to name our major life transitions or changes such as leaving home, divorces, deaths, babies, work and career changes. What did we learn? What helped us survive? And, to list some of our victories, defeats and regrets, and why we think they happened.

At the end we were asked to consider: If you have a purpose to being here on this planet at this time, what do you think it is and why?

"Does this feel like a graduate homework assignment or what?" Rebecca wailed.

I had to agree as I dropped the packet on my bed. "I wonder when we'll have the time to do this. Come on. Time to go check out everyone else."

Next door Linda was still unpacking. Veronica being the most Spartan of us, was already settled. She brought one small bag and everything was all put away and she was reading the agenda. She had a frown on her face and burst out with "This is invasive. I've never shared any of my history with anyone, including my ex-husband. What's the point? O.K., therapists, why do we have to do this?"

"Who knows?" I shrugged. "But, I'll bet Tanya will explain."

Linda was just starting to say something when Donna burst through the door.

"I'm outta here—this is outrageous. I'm not giving anyone this kind of information. How do I know what they'll do with it?" *Are all attorneys paranoid?* "This is too much!" She was stomping around the room waving her arms. She's a good venter. Her chest puffed up and she looked physically larger. I'd seen her do this successfully in the courtroom—it seemed to intimidate her opponents. Some of the women in our group were startled or put-off, but I was usually tickled by it, at least if it wasn't directed at me.

"Donna—come on, calm down. . . look," I pointed to the last two pages, "there's a statement of confidentiality and a waiver. I. . . "

"So what?" she stormed. "Like these mean anything?" She went on, explaining to the others how this could be used against us. I tuned her out.

My grandmother and my aunt trained me to toughen up, to be able to handle caustic energy. My aunt, especially, taught me that it's not bad for a woman to be angry. That anger can be a tool used to improve conditions for others, as well as not letting others step on your toes. Being direct, like a man, is called unfeminine, but these women taught me to be strong in the sense of being able to stand up for my rights, to say what I needed to say. My aunt has this incredible ability to sound so confident when she says something, that everyone believes her—no matter what. I too, am a master at faking people out—and doing it with style.

I just saw *Dolores Claiborne*. The best line in the movie goes: "Sometimes being a bitch is the only thing a woman has to hold on to." I take great delight in that line and have repeated it a lot. Women, for the most part, laugh. Men, even my husband, who usually gets women's humor, look uncomfortable. A woman who doesn't mind being labeled or called a bitch is very secure. So, I was affectionately thinking of my assertive and sometimes bitchy friends as I listened to Donna. I waited for her to run herself out, as I knew she would. Finally she stopped and I said. "You don't have to do it Donna. This is an opportunity to get to know yourself better and to share yourself with others. How far you go is up to you. It's O.K. to not do the exercise at all."

"Yeah, crap, I thought this was going to be a nice relaxing pleasant little vacation. Maybe I should go home." She was beginning to lose steam.

"I don't mind writing about my life so much but I sure don't want to share it with anyone," Veronica said.

One of the skills I learned growing up was peacekeeping. I found myself saying to both Veronica and Donna that it was their choice to do or not to do the work and they didn't have to decide right this minute. After all it was almost time for food. Ha! That got their attention.

"O.K., O.K., I'll table it for now. But, I don't like this whole thing. Where are they serving the food?" Donna was already heading toward the aromas of the kitchen.

As we walked by Gloria's room I poked my head in and asked if she was ready to get something to eat. Like myself, Miss Exercise Queen was always ready for food. She'd been laying on her bed, and as she swung her legs to the floor, she looked around.

"Isn't my room great?" She beamed. "I love the Victorian furniture and the colors. A teacup blue and violet comforter, the gorgeous paintings. And the bathroom," she sighed. "I could live there."

She joined us in the hallway, which was covered with original work from local artists. Skylights in the second story and a balcony overlooked the large living room. The staircase was creamy ash, and we wound around gently to the first floor where we skipped into the living room.

"I can smell food, good food," I hummed to the others.

"Yes, yes, yes, where is it?" Gloria caught up to where I was standing in the foyer trying to get my bearings.

Just then Tanya walked in. She led us through the kitchen and out to the sunroom. More flowers—petunias, marigolds and daisies were everywhere. Built-in comfy looking couches in earth tones with large green and blue pillows lined the windows which looked out onto backyard gardens. There was a built-in pond with a fountain and terraced gardens. I recognized several local plants, Purple Princess and rhododendrons.

"I'm in heaven," I said as I flopped on one of the couches.

Hors d'oeuvres filled the long wooden table in the middle of the room, along with coffee, tea, soft drinks and spring water. Platters of fruit, a vegetable tray and crackers and cheese, were artfully arranged.

Tanya left us with the explanation she'd see us after the snack for the opening session at 5:00 which would last two hours and then we'd have dinner. A nice sit-down dinner. Oh joy! We nibbled and snacked our way through the next twenty minutes, enjoying the sunroom, feeling cozy amidst a sprinkling of tension about what was to come. We were wondering about Joanna, the second instructor. I knew about her professional qualifications from her bio on the retreat brochure. The author of many books, and an international speaker and workshop leader, she was not known to me personally, and it was the personal I was interested in knowing about. I was also interested in her body movement background as I'd heard she practiced a form similar to what I used. Veronica has influential friends all over the world and had heard from an author/speaker friend of hers about Joanna.

"I hear she's brilliant and approachable. She's funny and loves to have a good time. He said if you read her books you get a good sense of who she is. She writes and speaks from her heart."

Good. She's not going to be one of those teachers who keeps themselves removed emotionally from their students. When I'm leading a workshop I prefer to get in and participate. I am less willing to give of myself as a student with a teacher that holds back from the group. I love to watch and learn how others teach with a co-teacher.

We finished eating and went to clean up as it was 4:30 and almost time for our first session. I was charged with electricity from the excitement and tension. So was Rebecca. "What do we think is going to happen?" she asked. "Baptism by fire? I've gone to lots of workshops, but I have a feeling this is going to be a lot more intimate—especially after looking at the questionnaire."

When we got to our room, I took five minutes to meditate and center myself for the meeting. Rebecca joined me. We sat in the rocking chairs, smiled at each other and turned our attention inward.

As I closed my eyes and began to breathe I became aware of my body sensations. The electrical charge was originating along my spine. I'd had this feeling before, especially just before I was going to make a leap of some kind, but never as powerfully as this. A picture of Joanna came into my mind's eye. She stood erect and tall, generating a rainbow of light and energy outwards in all directions. I was filled with a sense of peace and relaxation. I knew that whatever happened this week I would be O.K..

Chapter 7

Dusky afternoon sun slanted through the curtains, giving my room a rosy glow when I opened my eyes after meditating. I turned my head and looked across the room at Rebecca and willed her awake. I had to tell her about Joanna. She must've felt it, because she slowly opened her eyes, yawned and stretched.

"You awake?" I asked.

She rubbed her eyes. "Kind of. . . I guess. Why?"

I told her about my vision of Joanna and she said she had seen and felt something too.

"Wouldn't it be interesting if some of the others had a similar feeling?" I said.

"Maybe it was Joanna tuning in to us and helping us connect to her," said Rebecca pushing herself out of her rocker.

"Wouldn't that be great? I can't wait to meet her." I climbed out and headed to the bathroom.

We found our way to the meeting room which was in a separate wing of the house. It was floor to ceiling glass and looked out over the rolling hills with the ocean in the distant background. Breathtaking.

I didn't have time to ask if anyone else had had a vision because Tanya and Joanna walked in. The air seemed to shift, get more fluffy, as if the oxygen was expanding. I was in awe—something I protect against with teachers because I like to stay in my own power. Joanna hadn't even opened her mouth, but I knew her. She had on a long flowing rayon dress in shimmery blues. Her shoulder length silver hair, was pulled back with barrettes from her face, but full and wild on her neck. She had a strong widow's peak and was lightly tanned, wide-set eyes that crackled with intelligence, and a nose a little too big for her face. Her profile was regal.

"She definitely has presence," I whispered to Gloria who was seated next to me.

"She's incredible," Gloria agreed.

Tanya took a seat while Joanna remained standing with her back to the view of the ocean.

"I want to welcome you,"she began. "I'm so happy you're here and I look forward to all that we'll be sharing and experiencing together this week." Her voice was melodic and slightly husky, her smile genuine.

"For our first session I'd like to give us all an opportunity to get to know each other better by asking all of you to stand in a circle. One at a time we'll introduce ourselves to the group with a movement. No words, just a brief movement. It can be anything." We stood up and formed a circle. She nodded. "To give you an idea, though there is no right or wrong way to do this, I'll start." She proceeded to gracefully turn in a circle, rotating into the center of the circle and ending with a half curtsy and a bow of her head directed at all of us.

Gloria went next. She energetically marched into the center of the circle, did a couple of jumping jacks, laughed and marched out again. Another longish pause and Rebecca softly took a step into the center, opened her arms upward and folded them down into a prayer-like position, closed her eyes, opened them and moved back out into the circle.

Each movement gave everyone else a snapshot of who we saw ourselves to be and how we wanted to represent ourselves to each other. This was our first encounter with other women attending the retreat. A tall woman with silvery hair, I later learned was Laila, felt really uncomfortable doing the exercise and Joanna reminded her that she had permission to not participate. This seemed to free her up. She walked stiffly into the circle, covered her face with her hands, then placed her hands at her sides and walked backward into her place again.

A large full-bodied woman with dark hair pulled into a pony tail, her widows peak emphasizing her Native American features, strode to the center, caftan billowing around her. She knelt down, her arms stretched out in front of her and kissed the ground. Rachel appeared very strong and sure of herself.

Donna, surprised all of us with willingly stomping into the circle with her arms folded across her chest, grimacing, then smiling and stomping back to her place again.

Perfect, I thought, that's a perfect representation of how she feels to be here.

As the last woman finished we were all laughing and relaxed. What a wonderful ice-breaker.

Smiling, Joanna invited us to take our seats and she led us through the agenda for the week.

"As you know, this retreat is billed as the Greatest Change of All. By the end of the week, you will know what that is and it will be a different experience for each. All of you that have been attracted to this week are in a process of great change already. Whether you consciously know it or not, you are probably in the midst of the greatest change you'll ever go through in your lives.

"The significance of this is that these changes don't just affect your life, they affect all on the planet, as this planet readies itself for a shift from fear and violence to love and community." She paused to take a breath and turned to face the ocean, her back to us, blue swirls about her legs.

Loudly she continued. "In every generation there are way show-ers, those that create new frontiers. In past generations, adventurers like Columbus have sailed across the seas and discovered new worlds—in the physical world, beyond the known boundaries. But, now, the frontiers we must discover are internal. The exploration is of the inner territories of feelings, intuition, dreams, energy, spirit and even other planes of reality." She stretched her arms wide, pulling the ocean to her.

"The inner territory is more vast than the physical world and just as exciting. It is limitless. It is the path of the feminine to go inward. It is up to women to follow their calling and rise up to demand of themselves and of the men in their lives, that this inner re-balancing be accomplished for the good of all of us. There are men that are drawn to this path also, so when I say feminine, I'm not excluding men. Whether man or woman, the challenge is to merge the explorations of our inner world with the ability to live to the utmost in this physical world.

"Tanya and I will be facilitating your inner journey, giving you gentle encouragement as you go more deeply within yourself. We'll be holding the space for you to go as deeply within yourself as you're ready to experience. There are various tools we'll be utilizing to help accomplish this and we look forward to a wonderful growth-filled week together." She turned, more blue swirls, and opened her arms to us all as she sat down.

Tanya was up next, "Now that you know more about us and what to expect of the week, we'd like to give you a chance to introduce yourselves to each other and to get to know you better ourselves. Include what you hope to get out of this week. We'll do this popcorn style, so just speak when you're ready."

Usually I speak first to get my own stress out of the way. But, this time I deliberately sat, breathed and waited. I looked about the room at the four women I didn't know yet. Who are they and how will they affect our group?

A woman who looked to be in her sixties with beautiful light grey hair and a shy smile began. "My name is Laila and I'm very nervous. I've never done anything like this before and so I don't know what to expect. The questionnaire made me wonder why I came to this retreat. Yet, I know there must be a reason. I lost my husband about five years ago and haven't worked outside the home so I felt like I'd been thrust back into the world. I was so terrified the first two years I hardly know how I got through. I'm still scared, but the fear is more manageable. I'm so grateful for my children and the support of my women friends. I wouldn't have come to this if my friend, Ruth, hadn't convinced me. I need quiet time and don't want to feel like I have to do everything that's on the agenda."

She stopped and looked at Joanna. "What do I want to get out of this week? A chance to know myself better and be with other women. Time to reflect on where I'm going next in my life. I'm sixty-two, and I was planning on retiring and traveling with my husband. But, all that's changed and I don't know what I want to do or how to get there. I guess I'm hoping to clear some of the confusion that feels like cobwebs in my thinking. Thank-you." Laila bowed her head and didn't make eye contact with any of us.

I liked Laila immediately because of her honesty and because she carried my grandmother's name.

Joanna thanked Laila for speaking and let her know that taking care of herself and her needs was an important part of the week and that she could participate or not as she chose.

Ruth, with auburn hair and a short square body spoke up next. "I've wanted to come to a women's retreat for a long time. I used to say that my husband wouldn't let me do something like this, but it's not really true. I wouldn't let myself, and I blamed him. When I actually decided I was coming, he was fine. Oh, he grumbled and told me not to come back wearing hippie beads, but he was actually O.K. with the whole thing because I was.

"I'm excited about being here and what I'll discover about myself this week. I'm a teacher of junior high kids and have every summer off so I can de-stress and get ready for the next year. It's a demanding job, but I love it. I want to be more of a role model for the girls, who in seventh grade, really start to dampen themselves down so they'll fit in and so the boys will like them. It breaks my heart to see them do this. I think it'd be wonderful to have groups for young women or even retreats where they could get to know themselves better and focus more here," she pointed to her heart, "and not here," she pointed to her head.

"I want to be stimulated and learn new things about myself during this week. I also want to share and be with other women. I came to liking women later in life. My mother didn't have women friends and I've had a lot of male friends. Women didn't seem very interesting to me. I hated the way most women seemed more concerned with their make-up than with the state of the world. But, I'm beginning to change my mind about women and I've been enjoying my friendship with Laila very much over the last couple years." As Ruth finished she was beaming at the rest of us.

There was a pause. It was a little uncomfortable. Then Gloria said, "I've been in many groups with women and love being with women. I'm one of those women who have always had deep friendships with women and it's such a surprise when I hear that other women mistrust each other or backstab or don't think much of women in general. I'm still proud to be a feminist—not a femi-Nazi as Rush Limbaugh likes to impugn—but a woman who will defend other women, who feels good about her femininity while being able to hold her own in a world still mainly run by men." She gave a short laugh. "Don't get me wrong, I love men also but what I want to get out of this retreat is a deeper connection with women I already know, and a chance to know others. I want to give myself some much needed quiet time away from the demands of my professional life. I want to have fun and laugh and commune with all of you. That's enough. Thank-you." She met my gaze and smiled.

A striking blonde with big blue eyes, a full mouth and long, long legs, introduced herself next.

"My name is Joetta. Am I the youngest one here? I'm twenty-six," she drawled in a southern accent as she looked around the room and we all nodded. "I'm always the youngest woman in groups like these. Oh well. . . " she shrugged.

"I'm from Texas, if you're wondering about the accent. I'm excited to be here, nervous and worried about what y'all will think of me. I model—my looks are my living. Modeling is so competitive. I've made some good friends, but I've sure met some real ornery women, too. I like groups like these because they give me a chance to know other sides of women, beyond the competitive s-h-i-t that goes on in my work. I also want a chance to be known for what's inside me and not just for my looks." She smiled and looked to Joanna. Joanna nodded and thanked her.

I spoke next. "I'm thrilled to be here. I love women and think we're incredible. I love groups of women coming together and I know I'll get exactly what I need from this week. I want a deeper intimacy with myself and with you. It's scary to say that, because I know I tend to get what I ask for. I guess opening up to new parts of myself is worth the fear. I'm a therapist and do retreats for women. It's nice to come and be part of the process and not be in charge. What a gorgeous place. I already feel good here."

One by one we introduced ourselves. As each woman spoke of her pain, her life, her desires and her wishes for the week we began to form a bond that would grow and be nurtured each moment of the following days.

Joanna again stood and asked us to join her in a circle around a low coffee table covered in soft, paisley blue silk. We had been asked to bring an object from home that represents or symbolizes some aspect of ourselves. We were to place it on the altar. Not a religious altar, but a spiritual and feminine one meant to represent our group energy. It was a coming together of our energies. We were asked to place our objects when we felt moved to do so and to maintain silence.

As we began to place parts of ourselves on the altar, the energy in the room focused and whirled around each woman kneeling before the table deciding where to place her objects. Ruth carefully placed an arrangement of cards taped together facing outward. On these cards were animals, a beautiful mountain meadow, a mother holding a child and other scenes that showed us more about who she was.

As I moved forward to place my statue of Kuan Yin, the Chinese female goddess of compassion on the altar, I imagined and then seemed to feel her presence. I placed her at the back of the table looking out so she would spread her love over all of us. I also placed a small angel statue that usually hangs in my car and rings I wear from my grandmother and mother who both died two years ago. As I removed the rings from my fingers and placed them around Kuan Yin, tears dripped down my cheeks as I slipped into the shadowed emptiness their deaths have left with me.

One woman brought pictures of her husband and children, another a necklace that was special to her. Rachel's large physical presence spread out around her. She brought several objects that needed a large space on the altar. She had a hearty laugh and wore long loose brightly colored clothing with many necklaces of turquoise and amethyst draped around her neck. Bracelets of bone were thick on her wrists. As she moved, her jewelry jangled. Rocks, shells, crystals and feathers added to the picture forming of our group energy.

Joetta brought a Christmas tree angel with a beautiful face, made of cloth. She arranged sunflowers around it so artfully, it was mesmerizing. As the week unfolded she often showed this creative and colorful aspect of herself to the rest of us. Each symbol we brought to the altar would reveal itself in some way throughout the week.

When we finished, we silently admired the array of colors, scents and beauty. Joanna excused us for a two hour break which included dinner and then we were to reconvene at 8:30 for the evening program. I walked back to my room in silence. I was at peace. Even with the women I had just met, I felt safe and connected. I sat on my bed, breathing and smiling and happily being with me.

An hour and a half later, Rebecca and I were getting ready for dinner. She chose a turquoise tailored shirt tucked into perfectly fitting black shorts. I slipped into a soft cotton tank dress of muted earth tones.

"I loved the silent reverence we gave to each other when we placed our things on the altar," she said, fastening her earrings. "It reminded me of the best parts of the Catholic church when I was a girl. I used to love the chanting and beauty of the church, it was the dogma and hypocrisy I had trouble with, not to mention the attitudes towards women. Today, when I knelt down and arranged my things on the altar, I felt so loved and appreciated and I was appreciating myself. What a simple powerful experience!"

I smiled at her as I settled a rope of multi-colored beads around my neck. "I cherish the different ways we expressed ourselves. Wasn't that angel Joetta put out beautiful? I can't wait to get to know her better. I admire artistic people."

Rebecca was holding the door open. She had a dreamy look on her face. "Did you see how the whole altar took on character? I wonder how the week will play itself out. Come on, I'm starving and I bet there's something delicious being served. Don't you just love not cooking?"

"You have no idea just how much," I said.

"Yeah, right Taylor. Everyone knows Jim does all the cooking at your house!" Laughing, we headed to the dining room.

Chapter 8

At 7:00 p.m. we filed in and found our seats, the same seats we'd had earlier. I always find it interesting that once we've established our seating at school, the office, home, we usually maintain it, rigidly. When I was growing up my mother had "her chair" and no one had better sit in it. As an adult I did the same thing until I realized it was an odd thing to do. All the chairs of our kitchen set looked alike, what difference was it if one was at the end of the table or at the side?

As we got settled on the various couches and chairs and floor, Tanya began. "Our desire and hope for you is that you feel safe and comfortable here so you can more effortlessly explore deeper parts of yourselves. We wish to nurture you and give you time and space to nurture yourselves in ways we can so rarely do in our busy lives. This week is an unfolding and I look forward to being with you during the learning we'll all be doing together. If you choose to participate in an activity, great, if you choose not to, that is fine also. Check in with yourself and see what is best for you. I remember one retreat I attended a few years ago. I chose not to attend a number of events. Choosing was an act of power for myself, because normally I'd go along because I didn't want to miss out or because I thought someone might get mad at me if I didn't attend. This is your retreat and what you get out of it is up to you. I'll go over the logistics of basic house considerations and then Joanna and I will lead you through the next part of the program." She paused and looked around the room.

"We are many different women coming together. Some of us know each other and some don't. I want to encourage you to honor the differences and similarities each woman brings to this retreat. Quite often in society we use the differences—gender, race, economic status, and looks—to separate ourselves from each other. We invite you to notice the differences, discuss them if that's comfortable and embrace them. It's part of what gives each group a richness and wholeness. The similarities help us feel closer automatically and the differences help us stretch and grow."

Tanya went on for a few more minutes about house logistics and the agenda for the week. Then Joanna took over.

"Please get comfortable as I'll be leading you through a guided imagery to bring a sense of safety and comfort and introduce you to your Inner Advisor.

"Take a deep breath, all the way into your abdomen and as you exhale release any tension you don't need. . . .

"Continue to breathe and relax and let the couch or floor support your body, sink and melt into whatever you're sitting or lying upon. . . ." Rachel moved noisily, her skirts rustling, as she settled more deeply into her chair. I let out a sigh and relaxed as I allowed Joanna's voice to guide me.

"As you breathe you find yourself in a meadow with beautiful green grass and surrounded by trees. . . . You're walking on a dirt path and you notice many of your favorite flowers blooming along this path and in the meadow. You can smell the aroma of the flowers as the breeze gently moves along the tops of them. . . .

"You feel the sun on your face and the air is the perfect temperature for you." Joanna continued to guide us through a wonderful experience of going to a safe place of our choosing.

We were invited to create a symbol of our safe place by color and shape and then, imagining we could see, feel and sense the symbol, insert it, as if by magic, into our body. I placed mine in my solar plexus where feelings of anxiety or fear sometimes stir. Joanna then had us hold our hand on our body where we'd located our symbol and told us how we could re-access the feeling of safety anytime by laying our hand on this same spot again.

Joanna went on. "As you approach your Inner Advisor, notice how he or she looks, the light that surrounds her, the feeling you have as you move to stand in front of her. In what form has she appeared to you? An angel, mythical heroine or hero, some comical archetype?

"It doesn't matter, just have fun with the image

that presents itself to you and trust that this is the right one for you at this moment. . . .

"Greet your Inner Advisor. She wishes to speak to you and does so. Just listen. . . .

"If it feels like you're making the words up, let that be O.K. and just receive the information without judging it." Joanna paused for a few moments.

"Now notice she has her arms extended to you and is offering you a gift. It's unwrapped and let it be whatever first comes into your mind. This gift may be related to something you're to learn during this retreat. You accept the gift and say thank-you and good-bye for now. . . .

"Your Inner Advisor reminds you that she is available anytime for guidance and support. You only need to quiet yourself, come into the meadow and call upon her services. . . .

"Now as you come back along the path through the meadow, breathe deeply and bring with you whatever you need from this experience. Stretch your body and bring yourself fully back into the present moment."

After giving us a few minutes to stretch, Joanna continued.

"You'll notice the large sheets of paper and the various chalks, pencils, and crayons in baskets on the tables. Please take a sheet of paper and whatever colors appeal to you and let yourself draw something to represent the experience you just had."

In response to the groans of "I can't draw," Joanna added, "This isn't art class so we won't be grading anyone. You don't have to draw figures or anything that makes artistic sense. One way to experiment is to just place the colors you like on the page, let the color and your feelings guide you and continue until you feel complete."

"I hate this. I can't draw and don't want to," Donna burst forth abruptly.

"That's fine, Donna. There isn't any *have to*. Do what feels right to you," Tanya said gently.

The other women chose colors, and boldly or hesitantly, began to draw.

I wanted to capture the color of the Caribbean turquoise sea, where I envisioned my safe place. I like chalks because they blend so easily, so I chose blues and light browns with a couple of green colored ones for contrast. The gift I received from my Inner Advisor was a pink and green colored wand with a beautiful crystal on one end. The wand had to go in my drawing. I felt peaceful and centered as I drew. I wasn't sure how the wand would fit in but knew it was important.

It took about an hour for us to complete our drawings and share. By the time we were finished it was 10:00 p.m.—bedtime for me. I was exhausted, yet it was hard for me to leave the circle of chatting women. I always have this struggle. Should I pay attention to my needs—like sleep, or miss out on something?

I stood up to go back to my room, and felt a closeness that hadn't been present before our evening began. When Rebecca and Donna caught up with me, I was smiling as I headed to my room.

"How are you doing with this so far?" I asked as I put my arm around Donna's shoulder. "I know you don't much care for this touchy-feely stuff."

Donna shrugged me off. "I don't, but for some reason there is so much permission to not do the thing I don't want to do, that it's O.K.. And, I did like the imagery work. It was relaxing. I just didn't want to have to draw. Reminds me of being a kid in school and getting D's in art because I wanted to draw something different than my seventh grade art teacher wanted. Boy did we fight! I never want to go through that again," she moaned. "Here's my room. Night. . ." She walked through the doorway. "Be sure and pay attention to your dreams. I'll want a report in the morning."

"She's kidding, isn't she?" Rebecca laughed.

We walked into our rooms and I flopped onto my bed. "What a day. I'm pooped! Can't wait to see what happens tomorrow."

"Me either, but, right now, all I can think about is sleep." Rebecca looked at me thoughtfully. "My Inner Advisor gave me a jeweled box covered in diamonds—you know how I like diamonds—and the inside was covered with pink quilting. I knew that it being empty was perfect for now but at the end of the week I'd know what's inside." She pulled her Victoria Secret nightgown off the hook on the bathroom door. "I'll just be a minute."

Sitting up in bed, with the lights off, I quieted myself with my breath and gave thanks for the wonderful day. As I breathed more deeply, I called in my guides, Kuan Yin and the Archangels Raphael, Uriel, Gabriel and Michael for protection during the night, blessed them and also sent loving light to each of the women. Feeling grateful, I drifted off to sleep before Rebecca was even finished.

Chapter 9

I reached over to pound the alarm into silence but Rebecca beat me to it. She was already up and dressed.

"What time is it?" I moaned. "God, it can't be seven o'clock yet!"

"Well, it is and I'm on my way to walk with the others. See you at breakfast." She bounded out of the room.

I thought about going back to sleep, but headed for the shower instead. Not my normal routine. At home, I don't use an alarm clock. Mornings are when I meditate, write and take care of personal business. I may work late in the evening, but my mornings are blessedly open to my own scheduling.

By 7:50 I had meditated and was on my way to the sunroom to check out the yoga session. Tanya was a certified yoga instructor and I couldn't wait to do see what type she practiced.

Laila, Joetta, Linda and Ruth had all beat me there.
The "good morning—isn't this a beautiful day?"
evaporated on my lips as I saw Joetta was crying. The
others leaned towards her and listened intently. I joined
them.

"Oh, I had this awful dream last night. There was
a mean dark knight riding on a huge, ugly and powerful
horse. This horse had deformed growths all over its belly
and face and as the knight got closer he scared me to
death. I was in a dark forest filled with wet vines and
growth. I kept slipping, it was awful." She buried her head
in her hands. "The knight reached down to grab me and
I woke up. I was sweating and it was awful."

"Honey, you poor thing." Laila reached for her and
tried to take her in her arms, but Joetta pulled away and
Laila settled for holding her hand.

Tanya walked into the room, took in what was
happening and leaned down to speak to Joetta. "Bad
dream? Looks like it was an upsetting one."

Joetta took a deep breath and in a little girl voice
said, "I'm feeling better now. I don't want to interrupt the
yoga class. Can we just go on?" She straightened her back
and dabbed her nose with Kleenex.

"Of course. If you feel comfortable and want to
talk with me later, just let me know." Tanya motioned for
the rest of us to stand with her. "We'll start with the Sun
Salutation."

As I stretched with the others I wondered about
Joetta's overreaction to her nightmare. I refocused my
attention on Tanya as she led us through the Sun
Salutation, a moving yoga pose that requires upward

stretching and downward movement similar to push-ups. Laila did two of the postures and then sat with a grunt. "That's it for me. I can sure tell I'm out of shape."

"Do what you can, Laila," Tanya continued leading the rest of us and after five Sun Salutations we were all sweating lightly.

"Whew—I didn't know yoga was such a workout," panted Ruth.

Tanya then led us through a series of floor exercises that were designed to stretch our hips and legs.

We finished the class by lying on our backs, noticing our breath and quieting our minds. I was rejuvenated and anxious for breakfast. I glanced at Joetta. She grabbed a glass of water and flew out of the room.

"Joetta's still upset," I said to Laila and the others. "I wonder if it's just the dream."

"I think it's more," Ruth said as we made our way to the dining room. Fruits, cereals and yogurt, muffins and juices were artfully laid out. Vases of blush red and golden zinnias were intermingled amongst the food.

"Coffee, where's the coffee?" I rushed to the large coffee pot. "I hope the coffee is strong enough here." I sipped and smiled, "Ah. . . perfect!"

"Is it strong enough?" Gloria asked, as she poured herself a cup. She tasted it and beamed. "We love our stand-your-spoon-in-it-coffee, don't we Taylor?" We laughed as we took our seats with everyone else.

Joetta was noticeably absent at breakfast, but Rebecca, Donna, Rachel, Veronica and Gloria told us yoga students about their walk. "Joanna went with us this morning and she said there's a trail that goes for miles up the hills and into the National Forest. I'm going to take a long hike sometime this week. Anyone want to join me?" Veronica looked at Gloria.

"Sure. I love to hike for hours and hours," Gloria replied as she crunched on her granola covered fruit and yogurt. She wasn't one to miss any form of exercise—especially the strenuous type.

"I think something pretty serious is going on with Joetta," Ruth said. "I keep thinking about her and wondering how we can help."

"I'm sure we'll find out. For me, though, right now I want to enjoy my breakfast and all your wonderful company." I smiled at the group.

Ruth was startled and threw me a dark look. "Don't you care what's going on with her?"

"Of course I do, but I trust she'll share it when she can and my worrying about her only causes me to get upset, which I don't choose to do."

"But you're a therapist—you're supposed to care."

O.K., here we go. "Ruth, I do care. I've learned not to over-care because it's too hard on me and doesn't help anyone else. I guess I show my caring in a different way than you." I was leaning forward in my chair and my jaw was clenched tight. I felt criticized and took a deep breath and focused my attention on sending light and love through my heart to Ruth. I repeated a silent affirmation from *A Course in Miracles* to myself. I kept breathing and repeating it until I felt the tension lift out of my jaw and as I looked up at Ruth saw that she was looking at me with an odd expression in her eyes. She didn't say anything as she got up and put her dishes away.

Rebecca gave me a look that let me know she understood what had just happened. I knew we'd talk later.

The morning group started at 10:00 so I had a little time to myself. I went back to my room and laid on my bed reading one of the many books I always bring with me when I travel. This one was a mindless novel which was just what I needed to distract myself from thinking about Joetta or Ruth.

Rebecca waltzed into the room, singing to herself, and looking blonde and beautiful. "Oh, I feel good here in all this splendor. It's so nice to get away from my husband and clients and everything!" With a sparkle in her eyes, she kidded me. "I saw a little tension with Ruth. You bad uncaring therapist, you!"

I laughed and sat up. "Yeah. . . interesting, huh? One of the things I love about being with women is the 'stuff' that comes up. I've obviously pushed her buttons." I shrugged and Rebecca grinned at me.

I lost myself in my novel for half an hour until it was time to go to group.

The group was assembled in the meeting room as Rebecca and I entered; Joetta was absent. Ruth avoided eye contact as I sat down in a comfy rocking chair and pulled a soft white comforter over my legs and into my lap.

Tanya and Joanna walked into the room and greeted us with big smiles. Tanya was dressed casually in jeans and a light yellow sweatshirt with dancing women locked arm in arm across the front. Her hair was pulled up in a pony tail and she wore no visible make-up. Joanna had a flowing silk skirt and blouse in blended blues and violets. Blue seemed to be her color. Her hair was curled and her eyes radiated an intense blue with just enough eye shadow to bring out the color without distracting. Elegant and classy. Side by side, the two women were a contrast.

Tanya sat down as Joanna spoke to us. "This morning I'll be talking about change and the process of change. Then we'll do the first part of a movement exercise and break for lunch. When we come back this afternoon we'll finish the movement piece. Any questions?"

Ruth raised her hand. "I'm concerned about Joetta. Do either of you know what's going on with her?"

Tanya and Joanna looked at each other. "Joetta won't be with us this morning," Tanya said. "She's made the choice to just be with herself and see if she feels like joining us later."

Joanna nodded. "Whatever's going on with Joetta," she said, "let's send her loving thoughts and energy and trust that she'll work this out in her own way and share with us as she feels ready to do so."

"But shouldn't we do something?" Ruth stood up, dropping her folder onto the floor.

"There really isn't much for us to do Ruth," Joanna smiled. "If we all worry about Joetta what will that do to our energy levels? If we all try to do something to fix her, will it really have the desired effect on her? We women must learn to choose where to place our energies. Too often we leak our energy by worrying about someone or something that isn't our business."

"You sound like Taylor and I'm not sure what either of you mean. I feel like you're speaking a language I don't understand," Ruth said as she gathered her papers onto her lap.

"O.K., I think what we're trying to say is the only one that can really deal with Joetta is Joetta," Joanna told her. "As women we often exhaust ourselves worrying about others when it doesn't do any good anyway. On the other hand if we want to worry about Joetta, let's give ourselves some specific worry time. O.K., everyone, let's focus ourselves and worry for two minutes. Ready, set go!" She glanced at her watch. We were all confused, including me. "You're not worrying right!" she urged us.

We burst out laughing at how ridiculous worrying looked. Everyone but Ruth, who looked hurt and got up in tears and fled the room.

Joanna and Tanya watched her go. "Let her go. She needs to feel what's going on with her," Joanna told us. "Try not to get caught up in understanding this whole thing right now. I'll check in with you at the end of the day and see what awarenesses are different then. Let's get on with the idea of change for now."

Joanna began to talk about the topic of change and her perceptions of what change really means versus what we've been taught to believe it means. Everyone's attention gradually refocused from the drama of the previous few minutes, onto the topic at hand.

"Change is a part of life, isn't it? In fact, often times the only thing that is constant is that everything changes. Yet, most of us have habitual and often unconscious ways of handling the changes that go on in our lives. We react instead of choosing the response that best suits the moment. Think about the last big change that occurred in your life—a move, getting married, having a child, divorcing, retiring, a new job or career. How did you respond?" Joanna paused.

Gloria raised her hand.

"No need to raise your hand—we don't need to be formal with each other," Joanna kidded her.

"I remember just a few months ago I had a relationship break-up. I was devastated. I felt abandoned and depressed. I sank into a hole and isolated myself wondering if I'd ever have another relationship again. I blamed myself." Gloria looked miserable as she remembered the pain.

"Thank-you Gloria," Joanna said. "Anyone else?"

Rachel's high pitched voice rang out. "Yes, when we adopted our son a couple of years ago, I didn't realize how adding another member to our established couplehood would change the way my husband and I related to each other. In many ways realizing our dream of a family was wonderful, but it was also stressful. I was always criticizing my husband. Even though I feel I should have been more evolved than to act like a child, that's how I felt at times, like a big baby!" She chuckled as she shook her head.

"Great!" Joanna said. "What the two of you are talking about is your reactions to change. Change increases stress and when we're stressed we tend to revert to old behavior—even when we've moved beyond old reactionary ways of behaving. Anyone else?"

"During the first year of graduate school I felt as if everything I knew about myself disintegrated." I hadn't meant to speak yet, but did anyway. "It was the weirdest feeling. I didn't know who I was or where I was going. I cried and meditated a lot that first year. Gradually I became more comfortable with the intense emotional demands of the program." I let out a big sigh. "I'm glad to be on the finished side of graduate school."

Everyone nodded as Joanna continued. "Reactions to change vary don't they? And, none of our reactions are good or bad. They're survival mechanisms we've been taught by watching how our parents dealt with changes in their lives—gracefully or otherwise. As human beings we like to feel comfortable. Change creates discomfort, doesn't it?"

She turned towards me. "Taylor, at graduate school, you were a student again after being comfortable as a professional, earning money and feeling competent." Looking across the room, she said, "Gloria, when you broke up with your friend, your identity was changed from being a couple to being single and all that singlehood means to you.

"And Rachel brings up a good example of how even the most wonderful changes can create stress and cause uncomfortable reactions with which we have to deal creatively."

She was silent for a long moment, then she stood up. "Now we're going to do a Movement exercise that's designed to help you understand your particular style of reacting or responding to change. I'll explain it, demonstrate it and then lead you through it.

"This movement is called The Wave. Watch while I demonstrate with Tanya." With their sides turned to us, standing about two feet apart and facing each other, they extended their hands toward each other, connecting their palms. "The Wave is simply allowing your touching hands to move between the two of you like an ocean wave. Back and forth." They demonstrated for a minute or so and then Joanna said, "O.K., everyone please find a partner and begin."

We paired up. Linda and I stood up. Placing our palms together we began moving.

"This reminds me of movements we do in Aikido." Linda's rhythm was very slow and her touch was barely noticeable on my hands.

"I'm noticing I want more contact from you," I said. "I'd like you to press against my hands more. I feel like I have to press harder to get contact with you and then I feel like I'm being pushy."

"If I press harder, I feel like I'm being aggressive. I've never been good at confrontation. Maybe that's why it's hard for me to press against your hands? Wow, this is fascinating!"

"What I'm aware of is when I'm with someone who's a little quieter than I am, I feel pushy," I said, looking into Linda's deep blue eyes. "And, it's hard for me to ask for more time or to call and set social engagements because I'm afraid I'll be seen as pushy. Isn't this interesting?"

Tanya and Joanna moved around the room giving encouragement and observing our interactions. Tanya asked us to pay attention to how we started the movement and how we ended it and what happened in the middle.

Donna, paired up with Rachel, started laughing. "This is too weird. I don't feel anything. What am I supposed to be getting out of this?"

Rachel looked at Donna and said, "Are you uncomfortable touching another woman?"

"It's not a sexual thing, so no. And, don't start analyzing me, thank-you."

Rachel grinned. "I don't mean to analyze you. Let's see what we can learn about ourselves." Tanya had moved closer to Donna and Rachel and was observing them.

Donna started pushing more forcefully against Rachel's hands. Rachel's hands began to swing upward towards the ceiling with each movement toward her.

"Tanya, what's happening. I feel like I'm losing control." Rachel looked at Tanya, her face strained.

Donna just kept pushing away, ignoring Rachel's discomfort.

"Rachel, tell Donna what you're experiencing," Tanya suggested.

"I'm feeling pushed away from you and I feel like you're trying to be in control and not paying attention to how I'm feeling."

"Oh good grief," said Donna glaring at Rachel. "What?"

Tanya intervened. "Donna, I'm going to ask some questions. You don't have to answer them, but just think about them as you continue the movement. Don't judge yourself, just try to be an observer of your actions. Is there anything about the way you're doing the Wave movement that's familiar to you? Do you ever have situations in your life where people move away from you or say they feel pushed away?" Donna looked stricken. "If so, how does this behavior serve you and are there ways it doesn't serve you? Experiment with doing the Wave movement differently. Let Rachel be in charge for awhile. Slow your tempo down. Try a different pattern," Tanya said as she moved away.

Donna was flustered. "When you slow down I feel less frightened with you," Rachel said. "I feel like I want to keep doing this movement with you. Keep hanging out with you. What's going on with you?"

"I don't know, but I know I don't feel comfortable. Can we stop? I need to sit down for a minute and write some things down." Donna was sweating and uncomfortable. A flush crept up her neck and her usually expressive eyes were blank.

Joanna clapped her hands together. "Take a moment now to finish up and write down what you've discovered about yourself. Movement practices tap into our subconscious, similar to dream states, and the awareness often slips away if we don't anchor it in written form. Write about your feelings, body sensations, images, your interaction and feedback from your partner and anything else that stands out."

We scribbled for a good five minutes. "What a wonderful exercise!" Laila was excited. "I saw vividly how when I started the movement I was hesitant and slow and then, as each wave ended, I speeded up. That's exactly what happens when I'm working on a project. I have a hard time starting a project and then as the time it's due comes closer I start pushing harder. I procrastinate like crazy to start something. . . anything, from getting my car worked on to planting flowers in the garden. Then, I have to push really hard to get everything done. When I experimented doing the Wave differently I tried having more energy at the beginning and I didn't have to push so hard at the end. Maybe this is a cure for procrastination! Amazing!" Laila was thrilled and Rachel nodded as if she understood exactly.

"I start easily," Gloria said, "with a lot of energy, then fade off at the end. I have trouble finishing things I start. Well, some things, like paperwork, which I hate. But, how does this relate to change?"

"What was it like to do the Wave differently?" Tanya asked her.

Gloria grimaced. "Uncomfortable. It was awkward at first, but the more I kept doing the movement, the less uncomfortable it felt." She paused, then slapped her face. "Oh, I get it! So, if I want to change the way I'm doing something, say my paperwork, I could practice doing it differently and then it would feel more comfortable."

"How about you Donna?" Joanna asked. "Feel like talking about your experience?"

"This exercise was really uncomfortable because I realized my attorney pushiness is fine at work, but that in my personal life it keeps people away from me." Her dark eyes flashed. "I don't know how to do this differently. When I tried doing the movement differently I felt too vulnerable and had to quit. I do that with male relationships—someone starts getting too close and I end the relationship." She looked down.

Joanna's eyes warmly embraced each one of us. "Great work. This exercise is simple, but can touch very deep chords within us. Just let this information sit with you for awhile. It can be uncomfortable to see something new about ourselves. Try to be compassionate with your revelations. Anyone else want to share before we break for lunch?" Joanna asked.

Joetta walked into the room and quietly took a seat on the floor. Her eyes were red, her hair balled into a scrunchy on top of her head. Looking at the floor, she began to talk in a weak voice, "I would. . . I'm sorry if I caused any upset this morning. I thought I could come to this retreat and forget about my health problems, but I can't. Here, I'm feeling everything even more. I was diagnosed with cancer a few weeks ago. They said I have cancer of the cervix. The doctor wants to do a hysterectomy." She was speaking in a dull monotone. I hurt for her. "I've been having horrible periods for years and then for the last six months, one non-stop period. I kept putting off going to the doctor, and when I did they ran tests and oh, my God, I just can't believe it." She broke into tears, shielding her face with her hands. "I want children so badly and now that dream's destroyed."

Ruth ran over to her and put her arm around her shoulders. "Oh you poor kid. Have you had a second opinion? Aren't there any options besides surgery?"

Joanna stood in the center of the room, breathing deeply. "I'm sorry you're faced with such a health crisis and I'm so glad you're here. Perhaps there are some ways we can support you this week to prepare yourself. If you'd like we can also offer a healing circle several times throughout the week for you or anyone having health or other difficulties. Anyone else experienced in Reiki energy work?"

Rebecca, Linda and I raised our hands.

"Oh wonderful. What level are you?" she asked.

"Taylor and I are second degree and Linda is a Master," Rebecca told her.

"What's Reiki?" asked Rachel.

"It means spiritually guided life force energy," Joanna said. "It's energy from the universal or God force that is channeled through the healer but is not of the healer. Any one of you can learn to be channels for Reiki energy but you must be attuned by someone who is a Reiki Master. There are levels of attunement. First, second, third and in some systems up to the eighth level."

"I find that I use Reiki on myself a lot, especially when I feel stressed. I like to go to sleep with my hands over my heart. I can tell the energy is on because the palms of my hands get warm, sometimes real warm," I said.

With a glint in her eye, Rebecca said, "Tell 'em how you turn the energy on, Taylor."

"I hold my hands up, palms facing out and just say, 'Reiki on,'" I giggled. "Healing intention is what turns it on. It's so simple but the energy I feel in my hands is very powerful." I looked across at Joetta.

Joetta attempted a smile. "I don't know exactly what this Reiki is," she said, "but I'm willing to try anything if it will help me regain my health and not have surgery. Ever since I was a little girl I've wanted to have children and to think I may never be able to is too painful." She cried silently, her shoulders heaving.

Ruth held Joetta tightly and crooned to her. "Poor baby. There, there."

I was very uncomfortable with Ruth's caretaking, but decided not to say anything for now and see what happened.

Joanna spoke up. "This evening, Tanya and I want to invite you all to a healing circle at eight o'clock. Dress comfortably. Let's break for lunch."

"I've got to get outside for awhile. Anyone want to join me?" I said to the group as we left the meeting room.

"Sure. Let's take a walk and check out the grounds," Rachel said as she, Gloria and Veronica joined me.

"To be outside in the fresh air and glorious sunshine, ah. . . glorious sunshine. I guess that's a fairly rare event in this part of California. I love visiting but don't think I could ever live here," I said, filling my lungs. "I need the sun!" The girls chuckled in agreement, problems forgotten for the moment.

Chapter 10

We walked through the back door. A large hot tub bubbled and steamed. Green rolling hills, huge clumps of flowers and fragrant eucalyptus and pine trees along the walk ways and boundary of the property made my heart open and I breathed a long sigh. "Oh, this is heaven."

We walked silently, each with our own thoughts. Veronica interrupted the silence. "It's very odd for such a young woman as Joetta to have cervical cancer. I wonder what her family history is. Maybe I should ask her, see if she's open to another professional opinion." She looked thoughtful, then continued. "What exactly is Reiki energy? Do you guys really think it could help her?" I nodded, Veronica was so much more open to non-traditional treatments than she used to be.

"Are you familiar with the book by Dr. Larry Dosey called *Words That Heal*?" Veronica's brow furrowed and she shook her head no. "He's brought together scientific research from various sources that gives validity

107

to prayer and energy work as healing tools. I've used Reiki to heal my own health problems, like a stomach ache, or to speed the healing of a sprained ankle. I've also used it on Jim, with good results. He throws his back out periodically—usually when he's most stressed. While we're watching TV, I'll use Reiki energy on him. I increase the flow of energy by running my Light Body energy at the same time." I kept walking, bathed in colors and salty sea air mixed with eucalyptus.

"You're too much, Taylor. First Reiki, which I've never heard of, and now Light Body. What in the world is that?" Rachel blocked my path with her hands on her hips.

I bent to look closer at a purple and blue pansy. "Well. . . Light Body is a spiritual course that teaches how to balance our emotional, mental, physical and spiritual bodies. It's a series of classes and tapes. You take three weekend classes for each set of tapes and practice by listening to the tapes on your own. It's one of the most powerful programs I've ever experienced."

I stood up and looked into Rachel's face. "I was an atheist and into control—you know anal retentive—for so much of my life, this new way of thinking and being is amazing. The Light Body work has given me tools to use to balance myself emotionally, physically, mentally and spiritually when I feel whacked out. The other gift has been in helping me to manifest what I want and desire more accurately. I've been into creating what I want for years, but I was rather impotent, unfocused. The tools of meditation and Light Body helped me become focused. I love it!

"It's not for everyone. The shit hits the fan, so to speak, because as you learn to run the energy, to work with the power centers, unfinished emotional baggage comes to the surface. It comes to the surface to be healed. Sometimes I feel blissful while listening to a tape, other times uncomfortable, as stuff comes up. Discomfort is O.K.. My goal is to finish up in this lifetime, so I can go on to the next playground, whatever that means. We forget who we are when we're born into this lifetime and that we're these incredible spiritual beings who have come to learn about ourselves and each other. The forgetting can be too great a price to pay." I leaned over and stuck my nose into a pink rose with white edges that was almost fully open. "Umm, smells good. Sorry, didn't mean to lecture."

"Sure you didn't Taylor," Rachel said, laughing. "But, really, I didn't realize there were so many different paths and ways to explore spirituality. Kind of scary. My traditional Christian upbringing still makes me wonder if some of this might be of the dark side or the devil. How do I know it's not?"

Gloria, silent up to this point, spoke up. "By paying attention to whether it feels right to you or not. Taylor told me about the Light Body course and I listened to one of the tapes and it did nothing for me. But, obviously for her, it's been useful. We each have to tune in to what feels right for us."

Veronica who was marching along, trying to get us to pick up the pace, turned to Rachel. "I know what you mean, being raised a good Catholic I was taught to trust the Church. Anything not sanctioned by the Church was bad. The Light Body information is powerful and I love it, but the Church would say it's of the devil, bad, evil. But, then again, women were killed by the thousands, maybe millions for being healers, so-called witches."

She clenched her fists, "Makes me crazy when I think about it. I'm so frustrated with traditional medicine. I'm forced to see thirty patients a day for ten to fifteen minutes and I don't get to connect with most of them and really show that I care about them as human beings. They expect me to fix their symptoms by giving them a pill. Then, of course, there's the constant threat of lawsuits and malpractice. No wonder I take every weekend off and get out of town. It's the only way I can maintain my sanity." She was shaking her head as she fell in behind me.

We were nearing the top of a peaked hill covered with trees and brush. The view of the homes, hills and sea from above was spectacular. Birds were catching the thermals of rising warm air swirling off the hills. A hawk swooped toward us screeching. We stood in silence for quite a few minutes just appreciating the view, our connection to each other and to the beautiful surroundings.

"Nature is where I feel my spirit sing the most. I really enjoy Light Body and meditation, but nature is where I feel most centered and in touch with who I really am," Veronica said, gazing serenely out at the scene unfolding before us.

I squeezed Gloria hard and looked from her to Rachel. "Being with you here on this mountain feeds my soul. Sometimes I'm so alone. Going along this spiritual path I need and long for deeper connections with myself and my friends. I need to know that others understand what I'm going through. I need to know that even though we all have different ways of being with our inner selves, and with our spirituality, we honor each other's path. I'm so grateful for you in my life." I looked at each of them and lowered my eyes. I was kind of embarrassed to put my emotions out there like that. Hard to do. But each one of them looked back at me and I knew they understood. Without speaking we began our descent.

Lunch was set up on the deck. There was festive green salad with fancy greens, candied walnuts and feta cheese. Homemade scones were piled high. For those that wanted some extra protein there were cold cuts rolled and fanned on lettuce. Joetta was with us physically, but that was all. We allowed her to have her quiet space and didn't try to talk with her or draw her out.

After lunch there was free time and, wanting to be alone, I strolled back to my room. I sat in the rocking chair and faced the window with the shade up and the window open. I could look out on the lush foliage surrounding me and savor the fragrances of flowers and trees. The sky was pastel blue with shifting marshmallow clouds. I picked up my journal and wrote to sort out the feelings I was having.

I respect that we're all on our perfect paths and that I can love and bless someone but I can't change them. Joetta's illness frightened a part of me that feels vulnerable to the seemingly random manner in which disease strikes. Yet another part of me deep within my being knows there are no mistakes, and Joetta's illness is a friend to her. A friend to help her wake up to who she really is. A friend to help her heal some unhealed part of her being.

I started thinking about a book I read by Dannion Brinkley called *Saved By the Light*. He coined the term "great and powerful spiritual being" about us humans after he had a lengthy near-death experience. During that experience he was greeted on the other-side by Masters who reminded him that he was already a great and powerful spiritual being and that he, like most humans, had just forgotten. When I read his description of what a great and powerful spiritual being is I realized "I knew that, I already knew that." And, in five minutes forgot again!

I was inspired by Dannion's story and imagined how our human daily life might be when we all remember and are able, moment by moment, to live out of a state of love rather than fear. But, how and whether to share any of this with Joetta or with the group. What would be my motivation? To fix Joetta, to remind, to preach? As I sat breathing and asking for guidance these words began to form in my mind. I wrote:

We all become aware of our greatness, our unlimitedness in the perfect time for us. Just be who you are, share what you feel moved to share and trust that Joetta and all you come in contact with are blessed by your light and receive what is best for them at the time.

I yawned and stretched, and took a deep breath as I opened my eyes.

It was close to the time for the afternoon session. I gathered my notebook and water bottle and headed off to the meeting room. Everyone was there, chatting quietly among themselves. I felt so peaceful from my meditation, I floated over to one of the recliners and plopped myself down and waited, not wanting to talk to anyone, but to stay within my quietness.

Joanna and Tanya entered and Tanya told us what we'd be doing during the afternoon session. "Each of you had an experience with the Wave this morning. All of you are going through your own processes of change and we asked you to focus on one particular change to explore it more deeply. Laila is in a transition of going from not working to being a working woman and all that entails. Gloria is involved in starting a new business. Linda identified the shift she's experiencing with considering her needs as well as her family's." She acknowledged each woman with a barely perceptible nod.

"Some changes are brought about by our choices, others are imposed on us. The changes we choose are easier to handle then those imposed on us. Each time we're in a change process we go through the stages of beginning, middle and end. If someone is getting ready to move to a nicer home, and they made that choice, it's a positive change, right? It is certainly less stressful than if the move was motivated by another cause, say a spouse getting transferred unexpectedly. In fact, when stress assessments were made, moving was listed as one of the most stressful life events, right up there with divorce and the death of a loved one." She paused and settled deeper into the Lazy-Boy.

"The process of any move involves certain steps. First, you have to let go physically and emotionally.

There's an ending, a completion. Next you make the move. But, you're not immediately settled. It takes a few weeks or months and the time of moving and settling in is the middle, or the void. In the void you're still involved in letting go of the old house and getting settled in the new place. Everything seems up in the air. The details of settling in help to reestablish comfort and familiarity. In the move I just described, what do you think is the most uncomfortable time?" Tanya asked us.

"I think it's physically doing the move—like you said—leaving one home and not being established in the other." Laila was twisting a Kleenex between her hands and dabbing at her eyes with it. "After my husband died I moved out of the home we'd shared for thirty years. Thank God I had a lot of help to find a new place and do all the moving. I had to let go of a lot of accumulated stuff in that move. I must have cried buckets of tears as I went through drawers and found mementos my husband and I had shared over the years. I'm so relieved to be through that time."

Tanya encouraged her. "But the move was just part of the changes you were going through, wasn't it? You were also letting go of your husband, grieving for your life together and all the memories your home contained for you. I imagine you were also feeling the vacuum of the new life you were just beginning. You didn't know where your new life would take you or what it would involve. The void is filled with uncertainty and fear because we don't know what's coming. Our ego or personality likes to be in control, and when we're in fear we're reacting instead of responding." Joanna looked at Laila with so much warmth and compassion we knew she truly understood. "When I'm in a middle place, I find I have to meditate more to stay centered and if I don't, I tend to revert back to old patterns of impatience, temper tantrums, etc. Another difficulty with your situation, Laila, was that the changes you described weren't your choice. Your husband died. No wonder it was such a painful and difficult time."

"Thank-you," Laila said softly. "I became suicidal during that time. Today, I'm so much more clear about who I am and am learning how to support myself better and how to ask for help. I'm so grateful for my friend Ruth and other friends that have helped me endure. Now, I see the gifts of going through all that, but I sure couldn't then."

"That brings up a good point," Tanya said. "It's often when we are in the middle of a change time that we most need to be objective and step back from our emotional self, and it's the hardest time to do it. In intense fear, we go into survival mode. Surrendering the need to control allows us to see the bigger picture of growth, possibility and potential positive outcome."

"What do you mean surrender? I hear that word and it makes me crazy," Donna challenged making no attempt to hide the exasperation in her voice. "It sounds like giving up so how can that be helpful?"

"Good question, Donna." Joanna nodded her approval. "Surrender is a hard concept for Westerners to grasp. When I talk about surrender it doesn't mean giving up or giving in." She reached into a crystal vase and pulled out a small yellow rose. She held it out to us.

"Look at this rose bud. The next step in the bud's life is to open into a full flower, then to fade, wither and drop its petals, then to die. Every stage of its life is surrender to its purpose of becoming the flower. To imagine that the rosebud would resist its design and stop becoming a flower is silly. Why? It can't think, it just is. But, we think and that's both our gift and our curse. Thinking and over-analyzing gets in the way. We go from being in the flow of life, like a child, to being the in-control adult." She looked at our rapt faces, and smiled a little.

"Think about all the changes a young child goes through from birth to age five. Too many to count. The child embraces life's changes without thinking about it. She is in the flow of life. Why do you suppose change causes fear in adults?" Joanna's blue eyes narrowed. "By thinking, thinking, thinking. By the time a child reaches the age of seven and is in first grade the cognitive left side of the brain starts to be nurtured by school and learning. This isn't good or bad. We need to develop this part of our intelligence." She tapped her forefinger against her right temple. "But, what happens to the right side of the brain?"

"Our culture over-values the intellect and under-values the heart or emotions. We teach *doing* versus *being*. We need both. We admire people who are in charge and in control. We admire business owners who make lots of money. And believe me I have nothing against having lots of money. What I struggle with is the lack of balance that exists in each of us and in our culture."

She swung toward Donna. "To get back to your question, Donna, the process of surrender is natural to life until we attempt to control, or I should say, over-control life. The child is in the flow of life and moves from one event to the next without a lot of effort, in essence, in surrender to life. He doesn't think about whether to learn to talk, he just does. Nature is the same way. A tree doesn't stop and think, *hmm. . . is this a wise decision to go from a sapling to a tree?* It just does. Who's happier? Most children you see or most adults?" She stood quietly, arms crossed over her chest, eyes reflective.

Donna squirmed in her chair. "I understand what you're saying Joanna, but now I'm feeling I'm doing something wrong because I'm such a control freak."

"You and almost everyone else!" Joanna laughed. "I can't say this enough. This or anything we discuss or learn about this week is not about being right or wrong or good or bad. I say this so much because our cultural conditioning is strong and reinforces that if the teacher, or simply another person, disagrees with me, then I'm wrong. Not true, at least here. Don't struggle too much with this information. Let it sift through you and what you need to retain, you will." Donna nodded gently as she fingered the silver and malachite snakes dangling from her ears.

"We started this conversation because of discomfort with the word surrender. Let's have you experiment with surrender by doing the Wave again. Everyone please stand. This time as your partner comes toward you with her hands, experiment with surrendering to the movement that wants to happen."

Everyone stood and partnered up. I was with Donna this time. As I felt her hands coming towards me in the motion of the movement, I imagined being an ocean wave and allowing the pulse of the ocean to bring itself towards shore and recede again. I began to blend with the energy of the back and forth motion. Donna was concentrating very hard, there was a deep crease between her eyebrows.

"I'm going to get this," she insisted.

I continued the wave-like motion towards her and felt her tighten her arms against my incoming movement. I wanted to comment and give her suggestions on how to loosen up, but thought better of it.

"I'm imagining that I'm the ocean," I said, "and the great body of water is sending wave after wave to the shore in its own natural rhythm and as the wave I surrender to the incoming and then the outgoing motion. It's so peaceful. I have nothing to do, but just to allow. I am free."

Donna started to sputter. Then her expression changed and a spark came into her eye as her arms relaxed and an inkling of what I meant crept into her awareness. She became very absorbed in her movements. I moved my arms in different patterns, up and down and sideways and at first with each change she'd tense her arms again, but then she began to follow my lead and stopped resisting. Tears began to flow down her face. She tensed when the tears started and reverted back to trying to be in control of the movement. I didn't say a word. Joanna asked us to finish and write about our experiences before we discussed it as a group.

"Who would like to share what you experienced?" Tanya asked.

I shared my fantasy of being the ocean and feeling the pulse and melting into the perfection of each movement. "The sense of peace and freedom is still with me—in my body and my heart. I'd like to carry this back with me into my every day life. How do I do that?"

"Practice," Joanna said. "You've spent years learning how to not be in the flow of life and it takes practice, patience and time to re-learn. Hang out with children. They're great teachers." Everyone laughed, and nodded. It was so true.

Donna was still writing, absorbed in her thoughts, though the rest of us were noisily sharing our experiences with each other.

Veronica and Gloria had been paired and Gloria said, "At first Veronica and I had fun because we were both trying to be the leader. We laughed and didn't take the other too seriously. Then I had an awareness of how I can be in relationship sometimes. I like to be in control and sometimes I feel like if I'm not then I'm losing something of myself. Veronica and I experimented with sharing the leading and being O.K. with the follower role. I can see how getting more comfortable being the follower in this movement might help me be less controlling in my relationships."

Joanna raised an eyebrow and looked over at Veronica. "Do you feel like sharing how the experience was for you, Veronica?"

"Sure. I'm in charge in my work as a physician. I'm the oldest child of four siblings, so again I was in charge. In school I went for leadership roles. It's awkward to not feel in control, but there was a sense of relief also. Like I might be able to trust that someone else could do a competent job and I wouldn't have to do everything. Something I'll have to work on." She pushed her hair off her forehead again. "I'm so busy I don't have time for a relationship, but if and when I do, learning to trust in my partner's ability to lead would be good. In past relationships I got into power struggles and felt invaded if someone got too demanding with my time. The movement was a wonderful experience—not totally comfortable, but wonderful."

"Anyone else want to share before we break?" Tanya asked.

I looked at Donna to see if she might, but I couldn't catch her eye. I wanted to know what brought the tears. I'd never seen Donna cry.

Tanya uncoiled her long legs and stood up. "O.K., then, we'll meet again after lunch and an afternoon break. You all did so well. It's a joy for us to work with such a willing group. See you after the break." Tanya and Joanna moved off toward their section of the house.

Joetta was still sitting quietly talking with her partner Linda. They had their heads together and seemed unaware of anything going on around them. I was ready for some alone time so I headed off to the quiet of my room. My mind was filled with questions about Joetta, change, the Greatest Change of All. . . when would we get to it? Would some big revelation hit me on the last day? How could doing some relatively silly movement like the Wave bring up so many different insights and feelings? I'd have to ask some of these questions when we got together later.

Chapter 11

It was another meal from heaven—this time a free range roasted chicken with herbed rice and chanterelle mushrooms, lightly glazed carrots, tender-crisp green beans. Hmm, can't you just taste it? I was stuffed, but looking forward to the promised dessert—*crème brûlée*. The food here was as good as any of the best restaurants I'd been to in Mendocino.

We'd been asked to gather in a different meeting room located in the facilitator's wing of the home. Rebecca and I walked down the hallway, toward the murmur of voices. We entered a darkened room blazing with dozens of candles in varying heights. They were mostly white with groupings of violet and gold mixed in. Incense was thick in the air, as we found seats on the floor.

"Good evening. I hope you enjoyed your dinner. We had a special appearance from a chef friend of ours that used to work at Cafe Beaujolais. And, of course she also prepared the dessert for later." Tanya smiled widely, obviously happy to share that piece of gossip with us.

Rachel hurried in, late. "What's that smell?" she asked, her one-size-fits-all caftan billowing out behind her.

"Frankincense and myrrh," Joanna answered.

"Joanna," Rachel was fairly bursting. . ."the dinner was as good as Cafe B. What a treat. You are spoiling us and I love to be spoiled."

"Three cheers for the food," I prompted. Noisy cheers all around.

"Now, on to our evening session. This is a change of gears from earlier today and not something on the original agenda. However, listening to the voice of the feminine—to our instincts and where our heart directs us—means being open to following the flow of the moment.

"We have someone with us who is in pain and has graciously agreed to allow us to meditate and offer Reiki healing on her behalf this evening. We will lead you through a meditation preparing yourselves to receive healing energy and to direct it to Joetta. Whether you're trained in Reiki or not you can participate. Then we'll all sit in silence and allow the healing loving energy of the divine to find its natural course to wherever the healing needs to be for Joetta, and for all of us.

"It's hard to describe in words, but we want you just to have a sense of what will be happening. Please get comfortable and begin to breathe." She sat in the lotus posture and inhaled deeply. "Breathe into your abdomen and as you exhale release unnecessary thoughts or feelings you don't need in order to be present. Let the fullness of the dinner in your stomach take you deeply into yourselves and your connection with your higher power. Tanya and I will both be leading this evening and whichever of us feels directed to speak will." Joanna looked in Tanya's direction and she nodded in agreement.

"Those of you who know Reiki please begin to activate the energy," Tanya added.

I silently drew the symbols for second degree in the air in front of me, visualizing them in the color of violet as I'd been taught. Linda and Rebecca and our two leaders drew symbols in the air as well. The atmosphere in the room crackled with electrical energy. My thoughts became fewer and fewer as my body and mind relaxed more and more with each breath.

We all continued silently for a few more moments and then Joanna asked Joetta if she would mind allowing us to do some hands-on healing. She agreed. Joanna guided her to come into the center of the circle and she and Tanya placed their hands on her abdomen.

"Everyone just continue to breathe and imagine the light of the Divine, God, Goddess, All That Is flowing through you to wherever it is needed. No need to direct the energy consciously. It will find its needed place," Joanna intoned softly.

My body moved back and forth in rhythm with my breath and the pulse of the power I felt coming through me. The energy passed through the top of my head, my crown chakra, into my heart and out through my heart and my hands. My palms were warm, almost hot. I held them, palms out, towards Joetta lying on the floor. I was peaceful.

Tanya let us know it was time to start bringing our attention back into the room by feeling our body on the chair or couch and our feet on the floor. I thought only a few minutes had passed but the clock said it had been almost forty-five minutes.

We yawned and stretched. Joetta got up from the floor and went back to her place in the circle. She was silent and moved gingerly. Either she hurt or she was afraid she'd lose the healing magic if she moved abruptly.

Donna, as usual, brought us back to reality with a thud. "O.K., I went along with this because we do a meditation in our women's group at home. But, what's this supposed to do? Joetta do you feel any better? Is she healed, or what?"

Linda rolled her eyes. "Oh, please, let's give whatever we did a little time."

Joetta looked down at her hands which were gently clasped in her lap. Her voice was breathy. "I don't know what happened, but I feel spacey—out of focus. My stomach felt warm where Tanya and Joanna's hands were. I don't feel as afraid. . . but. . . I hope it helps me. . . " She trailed off.

Tanya interrupted before Donna could start grilling Joetta again. "Healing in this way is not necessarily instantaneous, though sometimes that happens, and it's not something we may see any physical signs of for quite a while, if ever. Healing requires trust that what is received is what is for the highest good. Speaking at a soul level, some of us have become ill in order to face ourselves in ways we wouldn't be able to do otherwise. As we do so we heal on many levels—emotionally, mentally, physically

124

and spiritually. Our soul often makes decisions that our ego—our personality self, isn't necessarily aware of." She met my eyes and I smiled. Isn't that the truth!

Tanya went on. "Let's trust that this work tonight is for Joetta's and all of our, highest good. Our ego wants to know now if 'it' worked, but our soul sees the larger picture and can help us relax into the not knowing. As we finish for this evening, Joanna and I invite you to maintain the silence we were just practicing. As you go into the hot tub or back to your rooms be quietly and gently with yourselves. Listen. Sense how you're feeling. Perhaps write or meditate or draw. We'll see you in the morning. Goodnight and bless you." Tanya picked up her belongings and she and Joanna walked over and hugged Joetta.

"What about dessert?" Ruth asked their retreating backs.

Joanna laughed, as she turned to face us. "It's ready in the kitchen along with herbal teas and fruit for those of you wanting something lighter. See what it's like to enjoy your desserts in silence."

"I don't know about this silence—especially while I'm eating something as incredible as *crème brûlée,*" Ruth complained, once our teachers had left.

The rest of us looked at her and nodded, but kept our mouths shut. I really wanted to just be by myself and, though normally the dessert would get my undivided attention, I decided to bypass it and take a bath. I was so filled with our meditation that the thought of food was too much. I wanted to use my time to work on the questionnaire from the first day.

Back upstairs, I ran my bath, added aromatic drops of foaming pikaki scented bath oil, dreamily removed my clothes and dropped into the tub. Bliss. Pikaki always reminds me of Hawaii and the ocean and the sense of freedom I have on the island. Eyes closed, I replayed the day. Home seemed far away. I missed Jim, but it was a warm snuggly feeling rather than the needy child longing I'd had in the early years of our relationship. I felt grateful for the time away and for the beauty of our surroundings and for the growing sense of friendship among us.

Twenty minutes later, I dried myself with the luxurious towels hanging on the door. I was content and ready to delve into the questionnaire. I pulled on my flannel pajamas and searched through my paperwork until I found what I was looking for. Seven pages, hmm. . . .

I settled into my rocker. Page one was basic information—family history, stories about birth and early childhood, my earliest memory, any recurring childhood nightmares. Pages two through four invited me to tell a short story about some event in my childhood that stood out, how I got along with siblings and peers and difficulties in childhood and adolescence, including successes and failures, any abuse, strengths and lessons learned. 'Seemed like a psychological evaluation and I thought that was rather strange, since this wasn't a graduate class for psychology, but a women's retreat.

When I was in my twenties and looked back on my childhood, I remembered a happy one filled with ventures into neighboring farmland, lots of animals that my mother allowed us to keep, roughhousing with my brother and sister, and having fun together.

In my thirties, as I was falling apart emotionally, I began to realize my happy childhood memories were true, but there was also a lot of pain I hadn't allowed myself to remember.

Now, in my forties, I can see the wholeness of my life to date and appreciate everything that's made me who I am. I ploughed through the questions on page one and felt some of the old feelings of fear, loneliness, and joy from my childhood. My dad's humor and silliness lightened up my mother's over-serious nature. Today, my dad's humor graces my life and I mostly share the silly side of myself with Jim. I've learned to temper my tendency to be too serious with lightness and I cherish my friends, like Rebecca, who make me laugh.

My adolescent years were hell. As I wrote about those years I grew tight through my solar plexus. There was one part of that time I hadn't been able to find peace with. That memory was the one I knew I would have the most difficulty sharing and I wondered if I would have the courage to do it.

I finished my writing and was contemplating it when Rebecca burst into the room. I hope I have half her energy when I turn fifty, I thought. Her eyes were sparkling and her cheeks glowed.

"Oh, great, you're still up. I was trying not to laugh because I thought you might be asleep. It looked like you wanted some time to yourself." She started taking off her coat and shoes.

"I did." I looked at my friend. How like her to be so considerate of my needs. "The meditation brought me more in touch with my quiet self and I wanted to start on this questionnaire. I usually find it hard to go off by myself in retreats because I don't want to miss anything," I laughed. "Did I miss anything?"

"Not a thing. We went for a short walk and then the others were going to go into the hot tub. The stars were right here tonight." She held her right hand up in front of her face. "Incredible!"

"Have you ever seen the stars in Santa Fe, New Mexico?" I asked. She shook her head no. "I remember walking out of a restaurant in the country and the stars met the ground. It was so magical, not a single tree to break the horizon."

Rebecca smiled dreamily and lay on her back on the bed. "You're working on the questionnaire, Taylor?"

"Yep, it's already bringing up feelings. Reminds me of the kind of stuff we did in grad school."

"Maybe you did, but at the school I attended we learned theories and didn't spend much time learning about ourselves. Most of my learning about myself has come through my co-dependency recovery and workshops I've gone to since school. I probably should start writing," she emphasized the *should* loudly, "but I don't feel like it tonight. I'm going to take a hot shower and hit the sack." She headed off for the bathroom, grabbing her robe on the way.

I put the paperwork away, turned off my light and snuggled deep into my covers. I was aware of lots of energy passing through the top of my head and gently sweeping through my body. I mentally envisioned the

Reiki symbols and placed one hand on my heart and the other on my abdomen sending nurturing energy to myself as I drifted off to sleep.

Chapter 12

We all met for breakfast. The morning was foggy and cold, as it so often is along the coast. I was bundled in warm cream colored sweats that helped me face the chill. I'm not a winter person. I love the ocean, but I wouldn't want to live on the northern California coast with those cold foggy mornings that sometimes stretch into days.

Growing up in southern California with not much seasonal change didn't prepare me for the colder winters of northern California and every year I go through a month or so of resistance to the coming winter. How's that for surrender, Tanya and Joanna? 'Lot of good the resistance does me as winter still finds its way to our valley every year.

I sat down next to Joetta who was by herself, head down, drinking coffee. She looked sad. "Great coffee, isn't it?"

"I'm just so embarrassed. I feel like people are waiting for me to give some kind of explanation." She shrugged her shoulders and disappeared into her huge caul-necked sweater.

I rubbed her hunched back gently. "We're just concerned and curious. But we also respect your privacy. I'm sure glad you're here though and you don't need to explain anything to me. I'm going to get some food—back in a minute." I was starving and found the array of usual breakfast offerings plus a hot tray of Eggs Benedict with spinach in place of the meat, with a sign that said it was made with low-fat ingredients.

Ruth and Laila were helping themselves and I joined them. "Isn't this a treat?"

"And, low-fat," Ruth winked. "Hard to believe tasty food can be good for you. I need a cook like this."

"I know," I said, grabbing a pink, linen napkin. "I think most of us have a secret or not-so-secret fantasy about having our own chef like Oprah does. Someone to cook low-fat, varied and incredible meals which are just waiting for us as we walk in the door. You know, like mothers did for our dads in the fifties and sixties."

"Or earlier," Laila reminded us. "I'm a bit older than you two."

"How's Joetta this morning? I saw you sitting next to her," Ruth whispered to me.

"She seems O.K.. Doesn't want to talk about 'it' still."

"When are we gonna get to know more about what's going on with her? I feel so sorry for her, Taylor." Ruth's face wrinkled with concern.

"When she's ready she'll tell us. We don't really need to know everything in order to support and love her."

"You sure are detached. How do you do that?" Laila asked me.

"Years of Alanon and practice. I get hooked once in awhile, but for the most part, I've had great teachers in my family who have taught me to detach and not focus on their problems, because when I did it made me upset and crazy. When I was struggling with my sister's last relapse, a counselor told me to remember she's on her perfect path. Everyone's on their perfect path and it's their life not mine. It's up to them to learn the lessons they came to learn and I need to stay out of it. She had me repeat the mantra 'She's on her perfect path' to distract myself. It's one I still use—like now with Joetta. I feel much more peaceful when I am willing to let go of the anxiety and worry." I left them and rejoined Joetta.

As we ate, I made idle chit chat with her. "It's so foggy this morning. I miss the sunshine. I guess I'm a sunshine addict."

"Hmm. . . I didn't even notice. I'm so wrapped up in myself I don't even know what's going on with anyone else. I'm scared, Taylor. Really scared," Joetta said, picking at her cranberry muffin.

"Of what?"

"I don't know what's going to happen to me." Her accent was getting stronger. "I thought cancer was something old people get. I'm too young to die. What've I done wrong to get it?"

133

"Don't blame yourself, Joetta. If there's some grand design to this, I don't believe it's to punish you. Maybe there's someone here who's had cancer and survived and can be of help. Everyone here wants to help. Will you let us?" I put my hand on top of hers for a moment.

Joetta blinked back tears and whispered, "I don't know how."

"You don't have to. Just admitting you want help and don't know how is a step. If you'd like me to, at the meeting this morning, I'll support you in anything you might want to share with the group. Is that O.K.?"

Tears rolled down her cheeks. "Thanks Taylor. I can see your clients are lucky to have you. Would you sit next to me? That would help." She paused. "I think I'm ready."

"Great! I have to go back for more Eggs Bennie. Want anything?"

A smile sneaked up on her. "More coffee, please."

Dishing up my second helping I noticed I felt very peaceful as I often do when I've been able to be of help to someone. Rebecca came in from her walk, her bangs plastered to her forehead.

"I love these foggy mornings." She piled her plate high.

"One of our differences—this is O.K. once in awhile, but I couldn't live here," I said.

"Really, God, I love it."

Joetta had left so Rebecca and I sat down and I caught her up on my talk with Joetta.

"Sounds like she opened up a bit to you. She must be feeling very alone. It's scary to admit we need people, that we need help. Being vulnerable isn't easy, but sometimes the pain is so bad we have to surrender control. You know about that, don't you?" Rebecca looked over at me tenderly.

"Oh, yeah. Like when my mom was dying of cancer, or my sister tried to take her life. It's a daily practice, and I don't have it down. When I'm in pain I sometimes forget how to take care of myself. I'm going to get ready for the morning session. I want to do at least part of my yoga and beauty routine before 10:00."

"And, how long does your routine normally take? I feel like I need to quit work just to have enough time to exercise, meditate and do my facial aerobics in the morning, not to mention spend time with my family." Rebecca puckered her lips, then pulled them back away from her teeth and stretched her neck upwards.

"That's lovely," I mimicked her movements and showed her one of mine where I kiss towards the ceiling. Gloria and Veronica were pointing at us and grinning.

"This exercise is to keep my face from falling down around my ankles," Rebecca told them. "Being fifty, I swore I'd never get a face lift, so I'm trying these facial gymnastics as an alternative. Oh, and I just ordered a device used by stroke patients. You hook it up to your lips and do this same movement. It's supposed to work wonders."

"I think the question is—can vanity and spirituality co-exist in our busy daily routines?" I quipped.

Rebecca threw up her hands in defeat. "I know! Each morning I spend at least two hours on all these things I do to get ready for the day and I'm having to get up earlier and earlier. Pretty soon I won't go to bed at all. I'll just start meditating about midnight and get up and work-out at 3:00 a.m. so I can finish my beauty routines and have time to write the book I'm always going to start. Am I addicted to self-improvement?"

"Yes, and so am I. But there are worse things to be addicted to. 'Gotta go. If we keep talking I'll never get to my morning ablutions." I marched off towards our room kissing the ceiling and chuckling.

Linda was excitedly comparing the Wave to her own massage techniques when we joined them forty-five minutes later. "I can't wait to get home to do the Wave with my husband. Won't it be interesting to see what happens? I'm so lucky, because he's so willing to try new things, even when he doesn't quite understand what it is or why."

"What do you think you'll discover?" I asked, schooching down next to her.

"I don't know for sure, but I'm imagining our patterns of relating will show up. Like, I initiate most things. . . get things going, and he follows. Unless it's sex, of course. He's better at keeping that part of our relationship going. And, I'm glad he does. At the end of the day I'm so tired and ready for bed I can let sex go for quite a while without his encouragement," she laughed, her exotic looks sharpened by her enthusiasm.

"What are we doing this morning?" Gloria asked.

"I'm not sure." I just hoped it wasn't something about the questionnaire. I wasn't feeling very introspective.

Gloria was full of questions. "What about Joetta? Wasn't last night wonderful? I slept so good and my dreams were incredible. I went to a beautiful temple of light in a place that felt like I imagine heaven would be and was shown a vision of my future by these incredible Beings of light. I don't remember the specifics of what they were teaching me, but I felt so peaceful and full of love and I have a sense they were trying to help me be more aware of my purpose here. I didn't want my dream to end. We were so happy to be together and in the light." Gloria had a distant, far away look in her eyes as she described her dream.

"You look like part of you is still in the dream, Gloria," I said.

"I'd like to be completely there. It was so peaceful. Do you think it's possible to create heaven on earth?"

"What do you mean? Like the heaven in the Bible?"

"I'm not sure, but I think I mean where we all feel loved and loving and there isn't violence or poverty. Where we all live in bliss."

I rested my face on my index finger. "Nah. . . not probable, but possible. I'm an optimist, but I doubt we'll live to see it. Let's just dream a little bit about what heaven on earth would be like."

Our conversation was interrupted as everyone found their way to their favorite seats. Joetta came in last looking more relaxed and even made eye contact with a few of us. She made her way over to me. We smiled at each other.

Most of the group members had their paperwork with them and some looked pretty uncomfortable. Donna was frowning as Rebecca and she talked.

Our fearless leaders moved effortlessly into the room. Both had skirts on, but that's where the similarity in style ended. Joanna's skirt was ankle length, a heavy cotton in blues with white threads weaving through horizontally. Tanya's skirt was bright red and of a lightweight silk or rayon. Both had on white, light weight sweaters. Joanna wore a beautiful southwest turquoise and silver necklace with matching earrings. Tanya had a couple of pins on her blouse. One was a violet purple and bright pink plastic looking square with a hand in the middle and another was a small silver hand with a cupped palm.

"You both have such interesting, unique jewelry," Rachel said. "I love to see what you'll be wearing each day."

Joanna smiled and fingered her necklace. "We've been to the southwest a lot doing workshops and retreats and it's the one place I love to shop. I always come back with some new piece of jewelry. I especially love Santa Fe, all kinds of original artists' works available."

Tanya faced us. "Welcome this morning. We had such a wonderful meditation last night. I imagine many of you had special dreams?"

A few of us raised our hands, or nodded.

"I find that just being away from home my dreams tend to be more intense—especially when I'm in retreat with other women. Anyone want to share your dreams?"

Gloria shared the dream she had told me about and then Laila spoke up.

"I had a dream about my husband last night. I haven't dreamt of him much at all in the last months. He came to me and held my hands and told me he was O.K. and not to worry, that he would be seeing me again. I didn't know what he meant by that." Laila shifted in her chair as if the groundedness of the chair would help her understand. "He didn't move his lips when he was talking but I knew everything he was saying. He kissed me goodbye and when he left I cried because I felt reassured. I woke from the dream with the tears on my face and a sense of contentment in my heart. I went back to a deep sleep. I'm not sure how to make sense of the dream though. Was it really him or was I just making it up?" Laila looked at the rest of us questioningly.

Joanna responded. "In one sense it doesn't really matter, does it? It looks like you feel relieved and more at peace with your husband's death."

Laila nodded.

"Some say that the veil between the world of the living and those that have gone to the other side isn't as great as we on the earth plane like to think. I've heard of many people being contacted by loved ones in their dreams and usually the dreams are reassurances from the deceased that they're O.K. and not to worry."

Joanna brought her hands together in front of her and then relaxed them at her sides. "Let's switch gears

139

now and check in with any concerns, feelings, or whatever you'd like to share about this morning. Then we'll move on to the questionnaire part of the process."

Joetta haltingly began. "I'm sorry to be such a baby. I'm so scared right now. So alone. I can see you all here but I feel like there's no way you can understand what I'm going through. I'm too young to be having cancer. I don't want this. I feel like I've done something wrong and am being punished. Maybe for being so pretty, or because. . . oh I don't know."

I sat next to her sending her love and miracles with my thoughts but not wanting to touch her to interrupt her feelings.

She reached out for my hand and I held it and gave her a gentle squeeze.

"It seems you want to be closer to the group. Is that true?" Tanya's eyebrows raised in question.

"But I don't know how." Joetta was very frustrated. "And I feel foolish and selfish. Foolish for being a baby and selfish for taking the group's time."

"Well, let's ask the group." She swept over us with her eyes. "Group, please honor how you really feel. Is it O.K. to give Joetta some time this morning?" Tanya asked us to raise our hands if it was not O.K.. No one did.

"Anything to get out of doing that questionnaire!" Donna put her hand to her forehead dramatically.

"Let's all sit in a circle on the floor—knee to knee," Joanna suggested.

We all moved to the floor. "What I'd like each of you to do is to go within yourselves for a few moments, listen to your deepest feelings, your inner voice of truth and then offer to the group some part of you or your history that seems right to share. This might be an old wound that still has an emotional charge to it, or an event that's unresolved. There's no *have to* with this, it's an invitation to reach deeply within yourself and take a risk. Take a few deep breaths and go within for a few moments."

This was the part I'd been dreading. Would my friends understand? More important, would they still accept me? I closed my eyes. God, I hoped so.

Chapter 13

Sounds of breathing and an occasional cough were the only noises as we shifted uncomfortably. Donna let out an audible groan. I started sweating lightly but kept breathing and going deep within myself. Immediately a picture of giving up my first child came into my mind. The same pain I always feel hit me, and an immediate desire to push it all away. This time it wouldn't go away.

I knew this memory would be the one I shared with the group. I dreaded the thought of feeling naked and exposed. Exposed to what? These are some of my dearest friends. Why should I be frightened to share anything with them? I guess I'm afraid of losing control emotionally and embarrassing myself. I kept breathing until Tanya called for our attention.

She was smiling. "Whoever wants to share first can do so when you're ready." She took a deep breath which reminded me that I was holding mine.

"O.K., I'm going to go first before I lose my nerve. Sharing emotional stuff is scary, but I always feel better afterwards." I twisted the string on my sweater. "During the summer, after I turned fifteen, my parents divorced. It was a horrible time for our family and to make it worse I knew I was pregnant. I'd been going with a boy the same age as I and got pregnant by him. I was in total denial I was having sex, so of course neither one of us used any form of protection. I knew the moment I conceived. We were out visiting the ranch where our family horse was boarded. We sneaked away from mom and dad and went off by the river. We made love quickly in the tall grass and warm sand and afterward I felt a fluttering warmth in my abdomen and I just knew I was probably pregnant. I didn't want to know, but I did.

"For the next seven months I pretended I didn't know. Through morning sickness, losing weight, and feeling horribly alone I kept my secret. My parents sold our home. My mother moved to be closer to her sister in another community. I started a different high school as a sophomore. I was about four months pregnant and skinny as a rail so I didn't show at all. I didn't tell my mother until I was seven months pregnant and just couldn't face going to school and continuing to deny the fact that my stomach was bulging through the girdle I'd been wearing.

"To this day I still find it hard to believe my mother or anyone close to me didn't guess that I was pregnant." I took a deep breath to calm myself, then went on.

"The pain I went through during those months of lying and pretending was awful. After I told my mother

144

and the school was informed, I had to leave school. I received home schooling from my teachers. They were kind, but I was mortified and humiliated and no one talked to me on an emotional level about how to cope with the feelings I was having."

A sob stuck in my throat. My tongue felt thick and fuzzy. I couldn't swallow or continue. Rebecca and Gloria who were on either side of me reached out to touch me.

"Immediately after I told my parents they made plans to get me to a physician and to logically convince me that giving the child up for adoption was the best course of action. I was so numb and yet relieved to not have to keep the secret I just went along with what they said. The physician I went to happened to know a young couple, a nurse and an engineer of the same coloring as I, that would love to adopt a baby. The arrangements were made. I never met them. I gave birth to my daughter under heavy anesthesia and never saw her, as that was also believed best. When I left the hospital, I went to my grandmother's and stayed for a week to physically heal. Nothing was discussed when I got back home. The unspoken message was everything is normal, everything is fine.

"I was a wreck. I had dabbled with drugs before I became pregnant and stopped while pregnant. I was in so much pain after giving my daughter up and didn't have a clue as to how to cope or deal with it. I found a new group of friends and started using drugs much more regularly. At one point, a few months after the birth, I called the doctor's office to try to find out about the baby before the six months waiting period was up. I was politely and gently told not to call back. My mother, who was drinking daily and barely keeping her job, just didn't have the energy or time to deal with me.

"I started running away for weekends to party with my friends and within six months of the first pregnancy I was pregnant again. Years later, a girlfriend said that when I told her about being pregnant that second time, I'd also told her that this time I was going to have something to show for it. I don't remember saying that, but it makes sense.

"One of the toughest things for me going through this experience was feeling like a social outcast. Most of what school friends I had backed off. I didn't even tell the one best friend from my old neighborhood, because I instinctively knew she wouldn't understand, then later when I had my son, she was judgmental towards me and didn't talk to me for a year or so. At times, I still have feelings of being left out that aren't based on what's true now, but on those old feelings. I've done a lot of work in therapy on these issues, but guess I just needed to share this with you. . . my friends. I feel closer to you after sharing, and I can tell by looking around that you care." I looked into Joetta's big blue eyes. They were wet as were mine.

"Part of the unfinished business from this part of my life is that I would like to locate my birth daughter. I want to and yet am terrified. I'm afraid she'll reject my efforts to get to know her on whatever level I can. I don't expect her to run to me with open arms, but hope that we can form some kind of relationship with each other over time. And, of course, I know I could never replace her true parents who are the ones that raised her."

Joanna looked at me and I felt her support flowing through her words. "Taylor," she said softly, "I'm so glad you decided to share this heartbreaking part of your life with us. I feel like I know you better and can see some of why I believe you are a wonderful therapist. Is there something we can do as a group to support you with what you've shared?"

I looked at the floor and grimaced as I wiped at my eyes. "You mean what do I need from you? I need help looking for my birth daughter. I've started before but I don't follow through and I need to do this. Maybe she needs me to do it for her. If I was a child who was given up for adoption—no matter what the circumstances—I bet I'd feel abandoned. I would appreciate it if once in awhile you'd ask me how the search is going and give me encouragement. When I find her I'll need some hand-holding and emotional support as I get ready to meet her. Afterwards I'll need you even more. I'm very afraid she won't want to see me."

I'd been sitting cross-legged and shifted to get more comfortable and to be able to look at each woman. "I've been told by psychics that we will reconnect and have a good relationship, so I'm hopeful. Thank-you so much for listening and supporting me." I sighed and hugged Rebecca and Gloria. Everyone came up one by one and gave me a hug. I was so relieved.

"Taylor's sharing may have struck an emotional chord in some of you," Joanna said. "Give yourselves time to say how you've been touched and then we'll move on to someone else."

"You strike me as so strong, so in control, Taylor, but you really had a tough time as a teenager," Laila said, touching her gray bun. "If I look at you as a professional, successful woman, then listen to your story of being pregnant at fifteen, it's hard for me to connect the two. You are strong, aren't you? I've heard stories about women who give their children up, but never from the woman herself. I really felt your pain as you talked. I hope you find your daughter, and if you need me, I'm here."

Donna was next. "I've known you for quite a while Taylor and this part of your life is a complete surprise to me. I'm sorry it's taken so long for you to share this and I don't know how to support you, except that I suppose I can offer legal advice if you need it." Donna looked at me intensely.

"Is there something else you want to ask me?" I asked.

"No." She paused, ran a hand over her face looking confused. "Maybe later." I met her eyes and nodded slightly.

I was amazed at the surprise of some of the women, but then I've lived with this story all these years. I have a tendency to keep it and the feelings stuffed so I forget that, it's, well, shocking. I felt drained so just sat back in my chair and rested as others responded.

Rachel had tears in her eyes. "My sister went into a home for unwed mothers when she got pregnant at seventeen. It was a huge secret in our family and everyone was pissed. She was sent away about five months into her pregnancy and came home a week after giving birth. She finished school, got married and had another child within two years. She wasn't happy though and still to this day she has problems forgiving herself for giving the child up. She hasn't been able to locate her little boy. I wasn't very nice to her when she came back. I was fourteen and embarrassed. To this day we've never been really close."

Rachel had her hair pulled severely back, making her widows' peak stand out. "Maybe I should try again. You've helped me understand a little bit of what she must have gone through."

"What does all this have to do with 'The Greatest Change?'" Gloria asked. "We've been here four days now and I'm not any more clear about what the big change is than I was when we first got here."

Joanna laughed, her turquoise earrings swinging. "See if you can hang out a bit more with wondering how all this fits together. We won't leave you hanging until you're walking out the door but we don't want to just give you the answers. Talk amongst yourselves, journal, ask for guidance and the answers will come."

"Let's go back into the quiet by closing our eyes and breathing and waiting to see what wants to emerge for our highest good." Joanna closed her eyes and began breathing.

Everyone followed suit. Soon I was restored and calm. What next?

I heard Joetta's barely audible voice. "When I was four the abuse started. My father would come into my bedroom after my mother had gone to bed and start stroking my hair and body. I woke up the first time and

149

thought what he was doing felt good and was O.K.. My daddy loves me, I thought.

"Every few nights he would come into my room after my mother went to bed. Then he started playing with my genitals—I knew that wasn't O.K.. It felt funny. I didn't like what he was doing. He told me not to tell mom, this was just our time together and she would be jealous.

"After a few weeks, he had me play with his penis and he'd masturbate. By the time I was six he was making me suck on his penis and he'd ejaculate in my mouth. I'd get so sick. He'd get angry with me if I didn't do what he said. He threatened he'd tell mommy that I was a bad girl, or that she'd want to give me away if I told, or she wouldn't believe me if I told her what he was doing.

"When I was only eight he started having intercourse with me. Not every time, once in awhile. He told me then he was helping me know how to please a man and that all daddy's taught their little girls to do this because they love them." Joetta was still. The silence was deep—we all hurt for her.

"I started having nightmares," she continued softly. "I gained weight and lost it and fell asleep in class. The teacher contacted my mother in second grade because she was concerned about me. My mother couldn't imagine what was wrong. Both my parents were into making sure things looked O.K. to the outside world. We lived in a nice neighborhood. My dad was a dentist and made lots of money. I had nice clothes and toys. Everything seemed perfect to everyone else. I wanted to die." Joetta's blonde hair was coming loose of the braid, framing her face which was white.

"When I was twelve I started my period and my dad stopped. I had a little sister so he started with her. I was so grateful he stopped hurting me, but I felt horrible and guilty that he was hurting her. I didn't know what to do. Finally, I told my mother. She refused to believe me, so nothing changed. I'll never understand that. God, I feel sick talking about this. I'm afraid to look at you. I want to die and just have the pain stop."

She stood up and strode to the window overlooking the back garden. "I've never told anyone besides a therapist. My sister and I have never discussed it. I don't see my parents very much and don't want to. Is it possible the sexual abuse and my cancer are related?" She spun around and looked pleadingly at Joanna.

Joanna walked over to Joetta, reached out and took her hand. "Well, it's possible," she said. "But, whether it is or isn't, the important thing is your healing."

Laila spoke up. "I was sexually molested as a child also." I looked over at Rebecca and she raised an eyebrow at me. "I've never told anyone. Listening to you brings up feelings I had almost forgotten. Maybe mine wasn't as bad as yours. It was an uncle and he never had intercourse with me. He would fondle me and have me touch his penis. This was my favorite uncle who would take me swimming when we kids went to visit them in the summer. I loved him. He was so much fun.

"Then, when I was about ten, he started touching me when he'd take me to the grocery store. I liked the attention and feeling special, but I didn't like him touching me. After the first time he touched me, I didn't like going back for visits, though we still had to. When I was about thirteen I told him to stop or I'd tell his wife. He did. I felt so lost and confused. I still feel the loss of the special relationship I had with him before he ruined it by touching me. Why do men do this?" Laila was crying and her friend Ruth reached out and hugged her.

"I guess this is truth time. How many of us here have been molested?" Tanya looked around the room, and of the twelve women in the room, five of us raised our hands, including Joanna.

A wave of voices floated across the room. "You see, many of us have had our trust betrayed by men or women we cared deeply about and felt cared for us," Joanna said. "It's not to say some of these men didn't care, but they didn't know how to be caring and not sexual. For other men, it's an issue of power and control. It's not just men who sexually abuse their loved ones or others, women do it too. Boys are molested as well, and they have an even more difficult time discussing it.

"It's an issue I've been trying to understand since my own abuse. I was a child of seven when a stranger came into our neighborhood and molested me one day. I tried to tell my mother afterwards, but she wouldn't believe me. I was devastated, and felt sick to death, so mom thought I had the flu and put me to bed. The next morning when I woke I didn't remember a thing. And, I didn't recall being molested until I began meditating in my early thirties, and the memories flooded back.

"When I hear about the repressed memory organizations trying to discount women's memories of abuse or trauma I want to scream. Some of us repress our memories, others deny them and still others have never been able to forget. But, people don't usually lie about being molested.

"In each retreat a quarter to half of the women have been molested or sexually traumatized in some way by someone they trusted. Anyone else feel like sharing?"

"I know sexual abuse is out there, but didn't realize how prevalent it is. It's scary. Why does it continue to happen? Why?" Gloria pleaded.

Joanna leaned in towards the group. "There are lots of explanations, but the one that makes the most sense to me is that for some reason some people believe it's O.K. to take what they want if they can. I think about men's sex drive and I know the politically correct version is that sexual abuse or molestation is an issue of power. I agree with that and see it as an issue of power over others. I also think there's more to it. Freud, with his drive theories, said that sex is our strongest drive. I think that's true for men. I don't think it's true for women, at least the women of whom I ask this question.

"I remember asking a good male friend of mine whether it's true he thinks of sex every ten seconds, as I'd heard some male therapist state jokingly that's how often men think of sex. This friend said, 'At least.' Then I asked a few more men how often they thought of sex. Some said they thought of it all the time, others many times a day. But in general, men thought about sex a lot more than the women in my informal survey. I don't think men are taught to manage their sexual energy in a healthy, respectful way. But, I'm getting way off track here, because I want to get back to you, Joetta. How are you doing now?" Joanna asked her gently.

"I'm glad to know I'm not the only one, but I feel awful. I feel sick to my stomach."

"Here, try smelling some of this peppermint aromatherapy oil. It soothes nausea. Put a drop on your solar plexus to release the emotional energy," Tanya offered.

Joetta held the container under her nose. "Umm, this smells so good."

We all got distracted as Tanya pulled out other aromatherapy samples and offered them around for us to smell and apply.

The mood in the room changed dramatically as we relaxed and had fun sniffing, oohing and aahing. "Wow, look! These oils are for emotional release. Tell us about them." Gloria was holding up a package of blended oils with names like 'release', 'forgiveness', 'hope', 'harmony'. "This is fascinating! How do they work?"

"Aromatherapy works on the principle that smelling is our strongest sense and that what we smell goes directly into the blood stream and to the brain. Some of the oils actually cross the blood-brain barrier and help to release trauma stored in the amygdala portion of the brain. The oils work on an energetic level, something to do with vibrational frequency, which I don't quite understand, and raising our frequency. I do know they support health because many of them are anti-bacterial, anti-fungal, anti-microbial, etc." Tanya held up the vials. "Help yourself, but for now, let's get back to our discussion."

"This is kind of strange, but since putting on the peppermint I feel better. Could it work that fast?" Joetta asked.

"Sure. They can move into the blood stream within three minutes. Oh, and one more thing about essential oils—the information about them is ancient. When King Tut's tomb was opened, among the gold and silver were hundreds of liters of oils such as frankincense and myrrh and lavender."

"I'm having a hard time concentrating because my butt is asleep and my stomach's growling. I need a break," I whined.

To the cacophony of yes's Tanya agreed. "Alright! What time is it? 12:30. Lunch time. No wonder you're so hungry and ready to change the pace. Let's meet back at 4:00. A few of you have requested a longer afternoon break so you can go into Mendocino. Is that good for everybody?"

Everyone murmured "yes" in response, or at least all I heard was a murmur because I was already on my way out the door to find lunch.

Chapter 14

"Hey, wait up." Veronica, Rebecca and Gloria were hot on my heels.

"You must be starved," Rebecca said, panting. "I just want you to know I think you telling your story was great, and I know it was hard for you."

Veronica moved closer to me as we walked. "I've known you all this time, yet you surprised me. I never knew you had experienced that kind of pain. I knew you came from the typical dysfunctional family, but. . . heck, you look so normal."

"Thanks Veronica. I appreciate that, but I'm ready to distract myself with eating. Then I'd like to take a walk. When the fog lifts it's gorgeous here, isn't it? I'm liking Mendocino better all the time."

In the lunch room, we were greeted by the biting smell of chili and a sweet cream of potato soup. Hot bread and rolls, fresh out of the oven, drinks, coffee, and nibbly vegetables were laid out.

We loaded our plates and sat down—small talk, laughing companionably and good food—great stuff.

Veronica broke the mood by asking about the Greatest Change.

"My curiosity is piqued but I imagine Joanna and Tanya will fill us in," Gloria said. "Or, we'll have to mutiny."

"What do you think this is, a ship?" Rebecca poked Gloria in the ribs.

"No, but you know what I mean. How long can they leave us in the dark? We've only got three more days!"

I waved my roll in the air as I brought it fully buttered to my mouth. "Patience is a virtue. But, actually, I'm sure by the time we leave we'll know what the Greatest Change of All is."

Veronica put her spoon down on the table and wrinkled her brow. "There are already a few clues. Let's think about this logically. What have we done since we got here?"

"Gained five pounds," Rebecca laughed.

"Besides that."

Gloria began reciting the week's accomplishments. "Well, we arrived and were thrilled by our beautiful surroundings. We received our packets of information, including the questionnaire. The first night we did that heartening and beautiful opening ritual. We were encouraged to draw to represent our experiences—which was new for me."

"And the change exercise. That must have something to do with it."

"Brilliant. But, what?" Veronica looked at Rebecca like she was missing the entire point.

Gloria was unperturbed. "Logically speaking, what did we experience from the change exercise? Hmm. The Wave made me realize how uncomfortable change is for me. And how much I like to be in control of anything, or, should I say, everything around me." She paused, contemplating. "I have a hard time trusting life. I don't know where this is coming from, but I'm aware right now, that I would like to be able to be less controlling with myself and with others. Know what I mean?" She looked at us.

"I can't relate at all," I said and we all laughed.

"So, is the Greatest Change of All about relaxing control and being in the flow of life more?" Rebecca asked.

"I think that's part of it," Veronica said. "I also became aware of my need to control my partner's movements and feeling uncomfortable with the idea of surrendering, which is like giving in to me. Then, in the middle of doing the Wave in a new way, I decided, what the hell, let's see what it feels like to flow rather than push. It was amazing! For just a moment, until I took charge again, I felt relaxed and. . . remember how we felt on the last day of school? Free? With nothing to do over the summer but play and goof off with our friends? That's what I felt like—and then, poof, it was gone."

"So what you're saying is similar to what Gloria said if we just look at the Wave exercise. Being in the flow of life is at least part of the Greatest Change of All, but, what's the rest?" I asked. "Let's ask some of the other women what they think it is. After we're done eating, of course. And, has anyone noticed what's for dessert?"

Rebecca headed over to the dessert table, beckoning me to follow. "There are lots of cookies on that table over by the coffee pot. They look homemade. Chocolate chip. You know my weakness for chocolate."

"Hey, bring some back for the rest of us," Veronica and Gloria yelled after us.

The chocolate was still warm; it stuck to my thumb. I licked it off, got a cup of coffee and went over to the table where Laila and Ruth were sitting with Linda and Joetta.

"May I join you ladies?" I asked.

"You're so formal. But, yes, please do." Linda smiled at me and motioned for me to sit next to her.

"Great timing Taylor." Joetta stood up. "I'm going to go to my room and rest for awhile. Thank-you all for your wonderful support. I can't believe people that barely know me can be so loving. I, uh. . .really appreciate it."

Joetta walked out and I sat down at the table. "We were sitting over there discussing what the Greatest Change of All is. It's almost the end of the retreat and it doesn't seem clear to me. What do you think it is?"

"You missed one." Linda pointed to my chin where a large crumb was trying to avoid being captured by my napkin.

I shared with them what Veronica and the rest of us had been discussing. "I've been wondering about it myself," Ruth admitted.

She went on. "It sounds like it should be big. Doesn't it sound like it should be dramatic, a major shift

160

of reality? I think the change exercise was very interesting, but it doesn't seem dramatic enough to be the Greatest Change of All, does it? What I learned about procrastinating was certainly helpful, but not life changing. Maybe I'm expecting too much."

"Part of the change I've felt this week is learning about some of the ways I interact with others. I've been so mad at you Taylor, for what looked to me like lack of caring for Joetta." Ruth's shoulders hunched over her coffee. "But, as I've thought about this and fumed over the week, I see there are different ways of showing that we care. In my family, to show you care, you do for people. If mom calls and needs something I've always expected myself to drop what I'm doing and deal with her needs, even though I may be grumbling under my breath. But, I'm not sure how this new awareness about myself is related to this big epiphany. There's Joanna, let's ask her." Ruth waved at Joanna and motioned her over.

"We've been discussing what the Greatest Change of All is and we're hoping you can help us figure it out." Ruth and the rest of us at the table proceeded to catch her up on our different perspectives and questions about what we'd been learning.

Joanna smiled and laughed. "Tanya and I have found it's best not to help you too much. You learn so much in the questioning process and if by the end of the week you truly need our help we'll be happy to accommodate you. You're on the right track. Keep talking with the others and try to keep an open mind wondering about the Greatest Change of All. Remember you can always meditate and ask for help from your guides as well. I'll see you at 4:00."

"Well, she wasn't much help!" Ruth complained. "I guess we'll have to work this out ourselves. But, everything is confusing right now. It's like I'm missing a piece of information that would pull everything together. It makes me nervous."

"For some reason, I feel trusting that we'll all come away with the right understanding or learning we're supposed to," I said.

Rebecca and Veronica came to my table with my purse and sweater. "Hey girlfriend, we're ready to go shopping and you're still eating. I know there are some wonderful shops in town just waiting for us to ravage them," Rebecca said, dropping my stuff onto the table in front of me.

"O.K. I'm ready. Let's go."

"This'll be fun. I can't wait to get out and see some of that cute little town," I said.

Veronica stretched her arms over her head and sighed. "I just want to get out. I'd like to find a bookstore and pick up a couple books Tanya told me about. If I see some white candles I might buy some of those or some incense. I really like the smell of frankincense and myrrh."

"And, I'm looking for clothes. You know me, I love new clothes and I haven't bought my seasonal ration yet." Rebecca had a dreamy look on her face as she got into the car and buckled up.

"What do you mean your ration? You always look elegant. I remember going to the movies with you one time. You said you were just wearing jeans. My idea of jeans and your idea of jeans were completely different. I came in my Levi button up jeans with a very casual shirt and Birkenstocks and you came dressed in high fashion jeans with belt, button-down shirt, your leather coat and cute little leather heels."

By this time we were blasting down the highway towards Mendocino. Rebecca and I were in the back and Veronica and Linda in the front carrying on about what the Greatest Change might be.

"Hey, any progress on the identifying what this change thing is?" I called from behind.

They were so engrossed in their conversation they didn't hear me. "I guess they'll fill us in later," I said, settling back against the seat.

We pulled off the main highway and came down the hill towards the town. Mendocino is set on a bluff that overlooks the ocean. We spent a few minutes searching for parking before one of us remembered to manifest a parking place by claiming out loud, "I am manifesting the perfect parking place now." Within about one minute someone pulled out of a space just in front of us and we zipped right into it.

"That always works," Linda said enthusiastically.

As we got out of the car we looked towards the south end of town, where the ocean was pounding up against the cliffs and spraying water halfway up their hundred foot heights.

"I love the smell of the ocean. Let me absorb this into my being. Ah. . . ," I noisily sniffed the air.

"Look where we parked," said Rebecca pointing to the dress shop in front of the car. The one we'd all been intending to visit. It was named Synchronicity. The shop was filled with brilliant batik cotton prints. Blouses, pants, jackets and skirts lined the aisles. The patterns on the materials were beautiful and Linda and I found ourselves looking at the same blouse with delight.

"Oh, a Goddess blouse. That violet is gorgeous. I have to get this." Linda looked at me.

"It's O.K. with me if it doesn't bother you, because I want it." I held the shirt up admiring it.

"Great. That'll be fun." Linda pulled hers off the rack, draped it over her arm and kept looking. I walked over to Rebecca and Veronica and showed them the blouse. They decided they had to have one also.

"Hey, what is this?" Linda asked when she saw them at the check stand with their blouses in hand.

"I know. I can't help myself. I love it!" Veronica replied.

"I don't think I've had girlfriends buy identical blouses since I was in Junior High," I teased. "I like it, it's kind of a bonding thing, isn't it?"

"We're just little girls at heart," Rebecca said making a face.

We continued along Ukiah Street, looking in the windows of the shops we passed, admiring the flowers planted by shopkeepers, as well as the ones that appeared to be volunteers.

"There's another clothing shop I'd like to check out just up the street. Let's keep going this direction." I motioned them along and we hurried up the block.

"Now, this is classy." Rebecca was running her hand amongst the racks of suits and dresses.

164

"Synchronicity has fun, weekend clothing and this store is more business oriented. Look at this pin, Linda." I held a pin up from the jacket it was attached to. The pin was brass and a metal that looked like silver. It was a human with caricature appendages and a hat on its head. "The legs move. Isn't it great?" I unpinned it and still looking, made my way towards the sales clerk.

Rebecca had found a lovely suit of blue wool with a short jacket and straight skirt.

"You'll look great in that, dah-ling," I complimented.

Linda and Veronica joined us at the counter and reminded us about stopping and getting some coffee before heading back to the retreat house.

After paying for our purchases we headed into a bakery with an espresso bar.

"Well, I'm not really hungry, but I could have a little something," I said, admiring the mouth-watering pastries, cookies, and rolls displayed in the glass case.

"I'm glad you're not hungry, because I can't imagine how any of us could ever be hungry again," Veronica said, rolling her eyes.

We sipped coffee and ate our bits of sweet rolls and cookies that we cut up to share. "I wonder what's for dinner?" I said with a buttery croissant in my mouth.

"What? Are you crazy? How can you think about dinner now?" Rebecca asked.

"Hey, when I'm on a trip and someone else is doing the cooking, I love to think and daydream about the next meal. It always makes Jim nuts too, but I think it's fun."

"It's a wonder you don't weigh five hundred pounds," Veronica said, reaching for a piece of rum-soaked pound cake.

"I used to, but, I don't binge or use it to satisfy other needs anymore."

Linda stopped chewing. "What do you mean?"

"I have reformed! Working with food addictions, I know that most of us food addicts get ordinary needs such as affection, attention, company, self-esteem mixed up and use food as a substitute. The sad thing is the feeling of comfort is so temporary. Kind of like an alcoholic or drug addict. The drink or the joint or whatever makes them feel better, but it's only a temporary fix. I've learned the hard way about why balance in my life is so important."

Rebecca made loud smacking noises, and held up a piece of pastry with yellow goo running over the edges. "Oh my God, this lemon one is scrumptious!"

"Are you trying to distract us off the subject?" I kidded her.

"Is it working?" She rolled her eyes.

"Shouldn't we start back?" Linda gathered her things and pushed her chair back, groaning as she stood up. We all laughed as we got our packages and headed out.

We left the rich smells of the bakery behind. "Hey, what were you and Veronica talking about on the way here? I couldn't hear from the backseat" I asked Veronica. Rebecca nodded.

"We were putting a couple of things together." Veronica stopped in the middle of the sidewalk. "Flow is important to the Greatest Change of All. The flow of life rather than trying to control and manage every minute detail."

Linda tucked a dark curl behind her ear. "And the flow of feelings is important. We need to accept that feelings are an important part of life. Like you said about the Wave, Taylor, feelings are part of the wave of life. Sometimes there are happy calm waves and sometimes there's a tidal wave that overwhelms us. However, the important thing is to ride the waves."

"Well said Linda!" Rebecca shifted her packages so she could open the door. "Reminds me of what Joanna said about change and how children and nature are such wonderful teachers for us."

Linda smiled and preened, pleased with the approval.

"O.K.. This is good. And, what else?" I demanded impatiently.

"Hey. . . patience, Taylor, we'll get it," Rebecca said.

We climbed into the van and while Linda started it up, I was struck again with the beauty of the ocean around Mendocino. Gulls were flying and squawking, clouds floated by in perfect formation and the air was tangy and wet.

"Do you think any miracles will occur for Donna?" Linda asked us as she pulled into traffic.

"Like what? That she decides there is a higher power? That would be a miracle," I laughed.

"I don't know, but I have this feeling something big is going to shift for her," Rebecca said.

I gazed out at the whitecaps and smiled. It's a miracle that I am alive and here to share this. Maybe that'll have to be enough.

Chapter 15

"It's ten minutes to four. Talk about getting the most out of our break," I said as we parked and ran quickly into the house.

I was sweating when I made it to the meeting room and I wondered if I'd be able to settle down and concentrate. I didn't feel like sitting still. I felt giddy. Maybe it's the sugar and caffeine. I scanned the room. Everyone was here.

Joanna stood up and moved to the center of the room. "I trust you all had a nice break. Anyone want to share what's going on before we continue with this afternoon's work. . . or should I say play?"

"I just want to say that I had a fun break and am not sure how I'm going to concentrate. Part of me is still in Mendocino shopping," I explained as Linda, Rebecca and Veronica exchanged glances.

Joanna laughed. "I think a centering exercise would be good. Let's have you close your eyes and get comfy."

"Breathe deeply into your abdomen and allow the tensions and distractions of the last couple of hours to melt away more and more each time you exhale. . . .

"Imagine you're in a safe and beautiful place. One that is entirely to your liking. The temperature is perfect, the sounds are nurturing and gentle, you can smell the pleasant aromas of the plants, water or earth. Just drink in the peace that exists here and the sense of relaxation as you fully allow yourself to be in your safe place. . . .

"The colors emanating from the sunlight embrace you with their warmth and cleanse each of the cells in your body and mind. Allow the color of rose to wash over you, then yellow, blue, green and finally violet. . . .

"Each color helps you become more aware of who you are and allows you to be settled within yourself. Breathe the colors deeply into every aspect of your being, allowing them to flow down and around you. . ." Joanna's voice emanated calmness and she let out a big sigh.

"Take a few moments to finish and when you're ready, breathe deeply again. . . feel your feet and wiggle your toes. . . allow your attention to come back into the room. . . ."

There was a gentle rustling as we re-entered the room. Joanna continued. "Please get out a piece of paper and draw a line down the middle, labeling one side A and one side B. Think of your best qualities, the way you most like people to see you and list those on the A side of the paper. List about ten or so. Then, looking at each adjective you placed on the A side, go to the B side and list its opposite."

This took a good half an hour. "Now, get together in pairs and discuss your reactions to the lists," Joanna directed us.

At the same time I was looking around, so was Rachel. We grinned at each other and I moved over to where she was sitting.

"Oh, good, Rachel, I haven't had a chance to be with you much this week. I liked listing my best qualities, but the opposites, I'm not so comfortable owning."

"I like the A list better, too, Taylor. For example, I said I'm direct, warm, motherly and funny. The opposites of indirect, cold, unmotherly or non-nurturing just aren't me. They're my mother. Oh my God! They are. The B list is my mother! I've deliberately tried not to model myself after her. I hate my mother." Rachel appeared to be in her fifties. In her agitation, she was pacing back and forth. Her large body seemed to enhance rather than detract from her grace and dignity.

I didn't want her to get upset, so I hurried on. "Let's see, on my A list, I wrote loving, happy, beautiful and successful, and their opposites are hateful, sad, ugly and failure. Nope, I'm not like any of my B list. And my mother wasn't either." We shared a look. "But something I fight against is being ugly, hateful or a failure. I hate those qualities. O.K., so what does it mean?"

The group was buzzing with "that's like me and that's not or could never be like me." Some were arguing and others laughing at themselves and each other.

"O.K., everyone," Tanya said. "Let's come back together and discuss what we've learned."

"The A list is perfect and the B list is obviously wrong," Rebecca announced.

Everyone laughed and Tanya encouraged other responses from us.

"I put nice on my A list and on the B list that turned into bitch. That's a word I don't like and I don't think of myself as one. I don't understand the point of this exercise." Laila appeared confused.

Gloria spoke up next. "On the A side I wrote peaceful and on the B side violent. Are you trying to say that the B side characteristics are us also? Because I'm not a violent person and work very hard not to be. Walking home from work one night with two bags of groceries, I was mugged and beaten. It was horrifying and I couldn't even defend myself. I was terrified and frozen. I just don't buy that I could be violent."

"The idea of being violent is repulsive to you, Gloria?" Joanna asked.

"Very!"

"When you read about violence or hear about it on the news, what's your reaction?"

"I don't watch the news or read the papers. I prefer to subject myself as little as possible to all the horrible things that go on in the world." Gloria wrinkled her face in distaste.

Rachel looked over at Gloria, "If someone threatened to harm one of my children, I could be violent."

"But, that's not violence," said Gloria as she looked up in surprise.

"Why not? If I shot the intruder, and I do keep a gun and I know how to use it, why wouldn't that be a violent act?" Rachel turned in her chair to face Gloria.

The energy in the room was intense. We were all pulled into the discussion. Joanna and Tanya sat calmly. I began to breathe deeply, a sure sign that emotional energy was rising.

"But your intention wouldn't have been to harm someone, but to protect. I think it's a completely different thing," Gloria said heatedly.

"I don't. I'm not saying I want to be violent or that I think it's O.K., but if I choose to defend my child or myself by shooting someone, I think I should call it what it is. You can't tell me there's no situation you can think of that could provoke you into violence?" Rachel's voice rose.

"Yes, I would fight to protect my child. But, I wouldn't call that violence, I'd call it protection."

"How would you protect your child, Gloria?" Tanya asked.

"I couldn't shoot anyone, but if I had a baseball bat I could use that, I suppose."

"And, what's not violent about that?" Rachel shot back.

Gloria's face contorted with anger and tears sprang to her eyes. "I don't understand this. I'm not a violent person and there's nothing any of you can say to make me think that defending myself is the same as being violent."

Joanna's voice was soft, kind. "I really want to thank you for being courageous enough to move into this discussion. This is a tough subject. It makes us

173

uncomfortable. What we're looking at with these lists is what's called The Shadow. The Shadow represents the unconscious or suppressed parts of ourselves, both personally and culturally. Women, in particular, have a tough time with this as we've bought into the gender distinctions that men are the ones with violent tendencies and women are the nurturers." Joanna sat for a moment, looking out at our faces.

"The Shadow can be a dangerous part of ourselves because it's the part we're afraid of. We push it into the deeper recesses of awareness and sometimes we block these parts out altogether. The way to freedom with the Shadow is to acknowledge it so it doesn't have to become a dragon to get our attention. What do some of you others think? Can you imagine situations where you might respond violently?"

I was sitting with my hand propped under my chin, fascinated, and considering my reactions to being violent.

"I don't know what I'd do if someone was hurting someone I love," I began, "but, I believe every one of us has the potential for violence, whether we're defending ourselves or someone we love. I think we women have a hard time thinking of ourselves in terms of being violent. We like to make our acts sound nice. But I agree with you Rachel, I think we should call it what it is. I know women are molesters, occasionally we murder, rob banks and commit other crimes of passion. We lie, cheat, steal and are imperfect just like men."

"Are you accusing us of lying and cheating Taylor?" Gloria screeched.

"No Gloria, but there are women who cheat, lie, steal, murder, and molest. We're not all nice and loving and nurturing."

Joanna interrupted. "As we can see, facing our collective Shadow is very uncomfortable. It brings up parts of our humanness we prefer to think belong to someone else. The importance of addressing the shadow aspects of ourselves is that it then has less power over us. Let's look at racism and ageism for a moment. Anyone here consider yourself racist?"

We all shook our heads.

"I think we're all somewhat racist in this society. I don't think we can help but be. And, I don't just mean we whites being racist about blacks or other cultures; I think it works both ways. But, to not admit our fear about other races actually keeps us more separate.

"I want to share a story with you." Joanna closed her eyes. "I attended a party when I was in my twenties. My husband and I were the only whites and our hosts warned us that one of her good friends who was coming was extremely racist. In my naïveté I hadn't thought about blacks being prejudiced.

When my husband and I came into the room I could tell right away which woman didn't like whites, she gave me a look of such disdain. I took it as my mission to get to know and understand that woman. We got into a good heated discussion and I think she could see I genuinely wanted to know how she felt. She made a good case for why she hated whites. I had to agree with many of her points. Slavery, blacks being treated unfairly for hundreds of years, and at that time still treated as second

175

class citizens. But one thing she couldn't explain to me. That was how her hatred of whites made her life any better.

At the end of the evening, I knew we would never be friends but we had a healthy respect for each other and shook hands and smiled as we parted. That night was a fascinating look at part of the American Shadow—racism. It takes courage to face the parts of ourselves we are afraid of. It pushes our growth edges and we become more compassionate with ourselves and others." Joanna opened her eyes, blinked and looked around the room.

She nodded slowly, "Now, let's move on with the exercise. The next piece I'd like you to do is to circle, on the B list, the qualities that most push your buttons. Of those circled pick one you'd like to focus on and then I'll explain what's next."

I circled bitch, helpless, and fool on my B list and finished by circling fool as the one to focus on.

"If you're all finished, please get a large piece of drawing paper and I want you to draw some representation of the quality you circled. You may feel moved to use certain colors or shapes without actually drawing an identifiable object. O.K., get started."

I moved over to where Rebecca was sitting. "Wow, this is some exercise, huh? I love it."

"I do too, but some don't. It's uncomfortable." She pulled two pieces of construction paper from the pile on the floor and handed me a piece.

"I picked fool to focus on, what'd you pick?"

"Anger," she growled at me.

What in the world could I draw? What is it I dislike about appearing foolish? I rolled my marker between my thumb and forefinger. Losing control, looking like I don't know what I'm doing and feeling like people don't like me. People pleasing, my old nemesis.

I drew myself in the center of a circle with people laughing and pointing their fingers at me. Yuk, this is awful. My solar plexus filled with tension and queasiness. But, if I'm feeling this strongly, this is the right way to draw this. I sat looking at my drawing and allowing the feelings to wash over me. Gradually, I became aware of the outer surroundings.

Next Tanya asked us to share how we felt about this part of the exercise.

Donna was fascinated. Actually doing it intrigued her much more than sitting around talking. "On my A list," she said, "I placed strong as one of my best qualities and on the B list, weak as a quality I hate. When you asked us to draw, a picture came to mind immediately. I tried to find another image or way to express weak with some strength to it and couldn't. This is what I drew."

She held up her drawing of a little girl with long brown hair, braided into two pigtails, with her head down, her arms limp along her sides and sitting in a room all by herself. "But, I don't know what this means."

"As uncomfortable as you are right now Donna, if you feel safe doing so, I'm going to ask you to hang out with the feelings and I think the next piece may help you become more clear about what this image means for you," Joanna said. "To continue this shadow exercise, what we'll do next is to act out the image you drew on the page. We

177

want to have everyone participate and support each other. Whoever is working gets to direct us as to how she would like our support. For example, Taylor, do you know how you would like us to help you dramatize what you drew?"

"Well. . . , " I thought for a moment, "I see myself first doing something foolish and then standing in the middle of all of you, having you point your fingers at me, gently please, and allowing myself to really feel the part of the fool. Sounds awful and wonderful at the same time."

"Are you ready to try it?" Joanna asked.

"Sure, in a few months. . . , " I said as I stood and everyone joined me.

"Whenever you're ready. Take your time and we'll take our cues from you. Does everyone understand your part?" She asked the others.

Everyone nodded.

I took a very deep breath. I didn't want to do anything funny, this felt important. I started walking around the room. All of a sudden I saw that it wasn't the part of the fool that pushed my buttons. The shamed and embarrassed pregnant teenager I had been loomed up once again. I shared this insight with the group. I asked them to point at me and use names that I had felt people were saying about me then. I told them that as a teenager, I had protected myself from names like "whore," "slut," with my wall of indifference. Everyone agreed to help me but was I really ready to live this over again? I shuddered and braced myself.

Chapter 16

Joanna gave a nod. I allowed myself to hear and take in the words "slut," "whore," "pregnant," "no-good," and phrases like "you can't be in school", "you got what you deserved", "who do you think you are"? My face caught fire, but I wouldn't allow myself to leave the room. My head down, I was deeply within myself. Then the voices stopped, I heard nothing. A rush of pleasant warmth surged upward from my pelvis to the top of my head and I opened my eyes to a roomful of loving, smiling, encouraging faces.

The shame had lifted, like a plug had been pulled and all that old negative energy was flushed out. Tears were streaming down my face and my nose was running. I can't remember a time when I felt so loved. Rebecca was the first to come forward and hug me. I hugged everyone, thanking these women—my friends. Tanya directed us, gently, to write in our journals.

I only wrote a few words. I was too caught up in the waves of energy pulsing through my body and mind. I was relaxed and as in love with myself as I was as a child of four.

"Who would like to go next?" Joanna asked, as we were shutting our journals.

"I can't believe I'm saying this, but I'd like to be next," Donna said.

"Great. How can we help you?" Tanya smiled. Her blonde ponytail rested on her right shoulder and like a golden rope pulled us toward her.

"I don't have a clue," Donna admitted, rubbing her palms together. She was nervous. I felt for her.

"How about if I make a suggestion and you see if it seems right to you?" Tanya offered.

"O.K."

"You could pretend you're a young girl, as in your drawing, and we could act out your parents, family members or teachers who talk to you and in movement and silent communication help you feel what your drawing portrays."

Donna thought for a moment and agreed to give it a try. "I feel really strange doing this, but I guess. . . I trust you all as much as I trust anyone."

"When you're ready just stand and allow your body to take you through posture into that little girl from your drawing," Joanna encouraged her.

Donna stood and took on a stance of fists up and jaw set. Her face dared us to come close.

As I looked at her I didn't see a tough woman. I saw a frightened, confused and neglected little girl. We began with the questions. "You look mad and I wonder what's making you so mad?" I said. "You're such a sweet little girl," Ruth told her gently, then voice after voice—"You look so sad." "What's making you feel so sad, sweetie?" "What's wrong?" "Would you like to tell us what's wrong?" "I'm here to listen to you. There's nothing weak about how you feel whether you're mad or sad."

The armored body posture melted as Donna, the little girl emerged. Head bowed, body pulled inward, big tears escaping from her eyes, she gave in.

Ruth moved to put a gentle arm around her shoulders as she started to pull away, then allowed herself to be embraced. Ruth held her and rubbed her back and talked to her softly. Donna pulled away. The whole thing had lasted less than five minutes, but we all felt the completion.

Joanna spoke. "Well done," she said, handing Donna a few tissues, and squeezed her hand. "Go ahead and journal for a few minutes and then we'll share."

Donna moved off by herself and wrote fast and furiously. I watched her jaw soften, her mouth relax.

Tanya opened the discussion. "Let's take about half an hour to share and then we'll break for dinner."

Hesitantly, finding her words, Donna spoke, "I feel weird, strange. I'm shook up inside, like I feel after a roller coaster ride. It's hard to find words. I think I was a sweet little girl in a family of boys who had to learn to defend herself or be crushed. I had three older brothers. I was the youngest and they were really hard on me. I guess I've always felt I had to be the toughest man around to

181

survive. The soft little girl part feels weird. I'm not sure I like her, yet."

Ruth reached out to her. "I was afraid you weren't going to let me comfort you. All I saw in the tough girl was the pain underneath. I'm sure you had to get tough to survive and I'm sure that serves you in your current profession. But there's a sweetness to you Donna, no matter how hard you try to hide it. . . and I like that part of you," she laughed.

I shared my observation about her face appearing softer and she was embarrassed.

"Soft or weak?" There was an edge to her voice.

"Soft doesn't necessarily mean weak, Donna," I said.

Joanna nodded. "What I'm hearing, Donna," she said, "is a confusion between weak and soft, as if the feminine part of you is somehow a weaker part. It sounds like in your family, as in our culture, the feminine characteristics weren't supported or were even put down and you had to disown those parts of yourself in order to survive."

Donna sniffed loudly. "I think this is all the touchy-feely stuff I can do for now." She stiffened up once again. I knew she'd need to really work on becoming comfortable with her softer side.

"I want to thank you for calling me names," I laughed, taking the attention off Donna. "At first it was horrible! But as I let myself go with the feelings it was like a wall within me melted and I had a rush of energy that was incredible. Wow! The therapist part of me knows that I got to complete a process that began when I was a teen and that I've kept away from myself by that wall of protection. I guess we both have our walls, don't we Donna?" I looked at her and she nodded. "This is really a powerful way to move through old stuck emotional baggage. Thanks. . . but I feel that familiar urge to eat. When do we break?"

Everyone laughed and the seriousness of the last couple of hours eased up as our attention moved to the dinner break and food—the great distractor!

"Let's go ahead and break for dinner. It's 7:00," Joanna said, glancing at her watch. "We'll meet again at 8:30 for guided imagery and meditation and we'll finish up the shadow work tomorrow."

When I got to the dining room Rebecca and Linda were already sitting at a table. I beelined over to them. I was so intent I almost didn't notice the table decorations, then I caught myself. A different flower arrangement every evening. Someone had an artistic hand. Tonight, in a gold pot stood a single delicate white orchid. I found myself smiling as I pulled out a chair. "I'm starving!" I announced.

"What's new?" Rebecca said. "I see you appreciating the orchid. I'd love to grow them, but I'm sure I'd kill it, as I do all indoor plants."

"You could just throw them away!" I said.

"What?" Rebecca looked shocked.

"Jim and I stayed at a Bed and Breakfast in San Francisco. I admired the orchids decorating the living room. I asked the owner how she cared for them, thinking she'd share her gardening secrets. She looked around to make sure her husband wasn't close and whispered that when they quit blooming she just threw them away."

Rebecca almost choked she laughed so hard.

"But more seriously, what was the shadow work like for you?" I redirected the conversation.

Gloria stretched her arms above her head and stifled a yawn. "I think what you did, Taylor, was gutsy. How do you feel? I'm tired and I didn't even share yet."

"I feel incredible. I feel more energized, lighter and blessedly more peaceful. Hope it lasts."

Veronica opened her mouth, closed it and finally said, "This work is almost too powerful. I don't know if I want to go where it's taking us."

We waited.

"On my first list I had intellectual and the opposite as dumb. But, I'm not dumb or stupid, so that's not quite the button for me. It's more like head versus heart. I'm scientifically oriented, I make judgements with my intellect most of the time. I'm comfortable there. Not so much with my feelings. And, frankly, I don't know if I want to go through whatever it would take for me to be more comfortable emotionally. I like the way I am."

Before any of us had a chance to respond, Joetta quietly walked into the room and made her way to our table. "May I join you?" Her troubled expression only made her more beautiful in a mysterious sort of way, as if she had a secret.

"Of course," I said, kicking a chair out to her. "Here. Feeling better?"

She sat down carefully. "I am. I feel like a puzzle that's finally had the last few pieces put together," she said. "I'm still raw, like the edges of the puzzle don't quite fit. I think just talking about the abuse and feeling so supported made me feel less alone. Don't know what this has got to do with the cancer or the Greatest Change of All," she shrugged. Unfortunately none of us could help her with that one.

Dinner was buffet style and I grabbed a warm plate. A line was already forming as the hot food was placed on the serving table. "This smells terrific," I said to Ruth who was in line ahead of me. Curried vegetable stew over rice called to me. A fruit salad sat next to a tossed salad of fancy greens topped with crumbled blue cheese. Smaller bowls of chopped peanuts, homemade plum chutney, coconut, olives, onions and chopped hard-boiled eggs were arranged next. For those who didn't care for curry there was a plain vegetable stew.

"Oh, I'm in heaven, once again," I said to Rebecca as she set her steaming plate next to mine.

Donna noisily slid a chair out across from us.

We ate in silent appreciation of one more fantastic meal and chit chatted about nothing in particular. I set my napkin down. "I know this shadow work is important to The Greatest Change of All. I read Robert Bly's work on the shadow and I loved it. He says we're born as whole complete golden globes of essence, but as we grow our parents try to civilize us. We learn parts of ourselves aren't acceptable. Like it's not O.K. to be angry. The price we pay for stuffing away parts of our authenticity is diminished energy and vitality for life and even illness." Donna hadn't said a word, but was listening intently. "He says in order to reclaim our vitality we must pull the forgotten or disowned parts of our self into the light and become more accepting of them."

"Does that mean Joetta brought her cancer on herself?" Donna stood up and crossed her arms over her chest, defiant.

"I'm not sure about any of it Donna. I'm trying to accept as much of myself as I can. The good and the bad. The light and the dark. I think it helps me accept others and I think it helps reduce stress."

"So we're supposed to accept the violent or murderous parts? That's a scary thought," Linda stated emphatically.

"Not *accept* necessarily, but maybe not deny completely," Rebecca said thoughtfully. "It's interesting that we have such a hard time accepting the idea that I, as an individual, can be violent, and yet, look at all the violence around us. More to the point is that if I can accept the possibility of my own rage I'm actually less likely to go off when something pushes my buttons. It's a paradoxical position. Accepting a part of the potential within ourselves doesn't mean we're giving approval for this behavior."

"I think this conversation is too heavy for me," Joetta said. "All I know is if my cancer is my fault, I'm sorry!" She jumped up.

Veronica grabbed her arm. "Don't run off. Stay with us. We're all trying to figure things out Joetta. Stay." Joetta slumped back down in her seat.

"I guess we'll have to await enlightenment," I said. "Maybe we'll get some insight during meditation later. Or from the dessert." I sniffed the air. "It's coming, I can smell something. . . apples?" Even Joetta perked up.

Trays of freshly baked apple crisp were brought into the room by the staff and placed on the buffet tables. We leaped from our chairs to help ourselves to the hot dessert.

"Look." Veronica pointed to the containers of freshly made vanilla ice cream. "It's going to be hard to go home and do my own cooking again," she groaned.

"I know. One of my fantasy goals is to have my own cook that will come in two or three times a week and make dinner for Jim and me and do dinner parties on occasion. Doesn't that sound rich?" I said, striking a rich lady pose, nose in the air, hand on hip. Veronica rolled her eyes. Joetta brushed past us.

"It's almost 8:00. I don't want to be late. I'll see you in the meeting room." Joetta had barely eaten her dessert and nodded to us as she placed her bowl in the kitchen cart, and left the room.

We watched her go. "She didn't have much to say, but at least she joined us and isn't just hanging out by herself in her room," Linda said.

"I feel something big going on inside her. She's been through a lot. It's wonderful she's so young and learning what she is so she can heal and get on with her life," I said, admiring the clump of ice cream on my spoon.

Linda clanged her bowl as her spoon hit bottom. "You think she's going to be O.K.?" she asked.

"I don't know why, but yes, I think she will." I finished up, dropped my bowl in the stack and headed to my bedroom, where I dropped onto my bed, and undid my jeans. I hope the Greatest Change isn't my weight. I grimaced as I rubbed my stomach. Relaxation with meditation and imagery, just what I needed to end a perfect day.

Chapter 17

The meditation room glowed softly. The shadows cast from dozens of candles, all white, but different sizes, blended with the now familiar aroma of frankincense. I sat down on a comfy cushion. I started to say something to Ruth, but she motioned to me to be quiet. No one was talking. Tanya and Joanna sat across from each other, eyes closed.

The silence lasted for another few minutes. Then Joanna spoke, "This evening we'd like to take you on a guided imagery journey to again meet your Inner Guidance or Higher Self. Use the term that fits for you. Allow your deeper wisdom to bring an image to you.

"Now, let us begin by getting comfortable and beginning to breathe more deeply and fully into your abdomen. As you exhale, allow any tensions to gently release with your breath. As you inhale, allow your breath to nurture and nourish all the cells in your body and mind and bring you to a more relaxed state. . . .

"Please affirm that any information you receive this evening is only that which is for your highest good. Let the sound of my voice take you more deeply within."

Someone coughed and another noisily adjusted her legs to get more comfortable. "As you continue to breathe and relax, you are transported to a higher plane of consciousness where colors are brighter and more vivid than on the earth plane, where you feel completely at peace, safe and protected. . . .

"At first you're only aware of beautiful rainbow colors flowing around you, as if you are in a mist of color, and then slowly, your vision clears and a temple of light appears in the background and becomes more clear as you move towards it. . . .

"You feel drawn, as if by a magnetic force, by the beauty of the light making up the structure of the temple. You glide up the many steps becoming aware the walls are not solid but are made of a liquid golden white light. . . ."

My breathing deepened and I let out a soft sigh as I relaxed even more with the imagery.

"As you get to the top of the stairs you enter a beautiful courtyard with a fountain in the middle and hundreds of fragrant white, yellow and orange flowers of many varieties. . . .

"You walk to the fountain and sit for a moment at the edge wondering about this place and what you are to receive here. . . .

"You breathe and continue to feel a deepening peace brought about by the flowers, the water and the soft tropical fresh air. . . .

"Then, a swirl of light moves from above and settles in one corner of the courtyard. This swirling light sparkles with clarity and you are curious about it. . . ."

Rebecca, sitting next to me, giggled. I peeked at her. She was beaming.

"The light begins to form an image and you find yourself looking at your Inner Guide, the one who is here to help you understand yourself better and is able to provide direction and guidance for the asking. You go and stand before your Guide and greet him or her. . . .

"Imagine your Guide's response, even if it feels like you're making it up. As you gain in experience in working with this energy you will feel more confident with listening and exchanging information with your Guide. Feel the love this Being has for you. . . .

"Sense the appreciation she has for your openness to explore and allow her to be with you and offer her wisdom and assistance. Perhaps you have a question you would like to ask. Go ahead and do so and again, see, sense or imagine her response. . . .

"As much as possible if the critic's voice or a feeling of judgement arises, just let it move through you like a puff of wind and come back to being present with your Guide and your dialogue. . . ."

A muffled "oh"and a cough distracted my attention back to the room and the people. I refocused by breathing and listening to Joanna once again.

"Your Guide finishes speaking with you. It's time for her to go now. You are filled with a feeling of love and acceptance for your Guide and for yourself. Allow yourself to bask in the light of this love for a moment. . . .

"Anchor this feeling into your body by placing your hands over your heart now and breathe deeply. . . .

"Thank your Guide for this meeting and remember you can visit again any time you choose by quieting yourself and taking this journey to the temple of light. Glance around as you leave the temple and walk down the steps. . . .

"Bring your awareness back from the higher planes of consciousness and begin to feel your physical body as you breathe deeply and feel your feet on the ground. Your attention brings you fully back into this present moment. Open your eyes when you are ready. . . ." Joanna let out a sigh as she completed the journey.

We all stretched, groaned and moved around. I felt very relaxed and ready for bed. I moved my legs out from under me as did Rebecca. Our legs collided. We giggled. I mouthed "Move over." She ignored me.

Ruth was first to speak. "What a wonderful journey. We did that one guided journey a few days ago, and I didn't really see or sense anything. But this time I actually felt like I was in the presence of a high Being. That I was loved. That had my best interests in mind. I feel great. I feel I made a connection that I don't want to lose. How can I do this at home?"

"There are many ways to connect with inner or higher guidance. And, basically, it's practice, practice, practice," Joanna said. "Spending quiet time on a daily basis at a regular time helps our body and our mind build a connection. Inner journeys like this are only one way to connect to guidance. Some feel a connection to their Guides in meditation or out in nature. There is no one way because we're all wonderful and unique beings. Just practice in a fun light way when you're meditating or having quiet time and be patient as it can take awhile to develop this relationship with your Higher Self. I'm so glad you enjoyed the journey."

"My guide looked like my husband. Is that O.K.?" Laila asked.

"Of course, if it felt like a loving caring guide and not one that's critical or judgmental," Tanya said.

"But, shouldn't my guide be a higher form than my husband? I loved him and think he was a special man, but. . . " Laila's brow furrowed, her eyes intent.

Tanya responded to her. "Sometimes the higher, wiser parts of ourselves use symbols that we'll feel most comfortable with, and that may be why you saw an image of your husband. My guides have changed form over the years as I have grown and evolved. Yours probably will too. Have fun with the imagery. Use it as a tool and if some piece of information doesn't feel right or seems out of context, wait and see how it feels over time. Just remember to do the protection affirmation, 'I close my aura to all except my own I AM presence and affirm only that which is for my highest good occurs'. I find it makes me feel more trusting of the information I get."

Joanna nodded. "Anyone else want to share before we finish for the evening?" she asked.

"I do," I said. "In the first imagery we did at the beginning of the retreat, I received a wand from my Guide. Tonight I had the wand in my hand and used it to fly about the courtyard and then I just took off into the Universe and flew with the stars and my Guide laughing and having fun. I felt like I could do anything I wished. I had a feeling of all possibilities being open to me. I was joined by some of you! Rebecca, you were there. We played like children. Donna, you were there." She wrinkled her face at me. "I wish I could bring that freedom and fun into my everyday life," I said.

"I know exactly what you mean Taylor," Rachel said. "Two more days and we leave and go back to reality. I can already feel my everyday life beginning to pull at me and I'm not ready. During the imagery, I felt angelic presences around me. I was accepted and safe. I knew that everything that happened in the journey and in life would be O.K.. I so want to remember what I'm learning. I don't want to forget everything in the busyness of work, kids, projects—you know. My shoulders are tightening and some of the peace of the last few days is evaporating. Help Joanna and Tanya! I don't want to lose this sense of grace when I return home." Everyone laughed nervously, looking at our leaders—could they help us?

"I hadn't even thought of how it will be to make the transition back to real life. Thanks for bringing it up," said Rebecca as she sat up straighter. "In the journey I had a picture of my heart and my mind and how the two were beginning to build a bridge between each other. As the bridge connected I felt more whole, centered and in touch with my higher nature than I ever have. I wish I could describe the power of the image and the feeling, but words seem inadequate."

Tanya turned her attention to Rachel. "I think you used the word grace. There seems to be a theme of not wanting to lose the peace and connection with your

Higher Self you're establishing. Something we hear at every retreat about this time during the week is a sense of wondering or even anxiety about how to maintain at least some of this grace or peace in your everyday lives. I want to encourage all of you to write down a few ideas you have about how to support your spiritual selves every day no matter how busy or hectic your lives are. We'll talk more about how to do this on the last day."

Joanna grinned at her and spoke, "You are all Great and Powerful Spiritual Beings and it is a gift to be with you during this week. Have wonderful dreams and we'll see you in the morning." Our spiritual evening ended with a thud.

My legs were stiff as I pushed myself up and gathered my notebook and water bottle. It was 9:30 and I was ready for sleep. Rebecca joined me and we walked slowly to our room.

"I really need some time to myself Rebecca. Just to be quiet and assimilate all that's happened today. Is that O.K.?"

"Me too. Goodnight." Rebecca opened the door and we quietly went about getting ready for bed.

Later, in bed, I listened to the night sounds of frogs and crickets. I glanced out to look at the stars. It was clear and a shooting star swung wide across the black sky. "Did you see that Rebecca?" I whispered.

"Shhh. . . you're not supposed to talk," she laughed. "What a nightcap—a shooting star. Make a wish and I'll see you in the morning."

I yawned and scrunched down into my covers. Make a wish, what do I wish for? Help in maintaining this peace and at-one-ment I'm feeling tonight and a way to bring it home with me.

Chapter 18

At ten o'clock the next morning we gathered in the meeting room. The room was filled with fresh flowers and sunny morning air. I saw Joetta come into the room and I waved for her to come over and sit with me.

"Well, you look good this morning. Sleep well?" I asked.

"I haven't felt this good in months and months." She practically beamed. "I had an incredible dream. I want to tell the whole group. Something inside me has changed. I'm stirred up, excited and unsure all at the same time." She closed her eyes for a moment, searching for words. "A deep cleansing has been going on inside me during this week, and I'm definitely different."

I squeezed her hand, and she rewarded me with a brilliant smile.

The rest of the women arrived and began to settle into their designated spots. Joanna and Tanya were already in the room looking at notes and talking softly to each other.

"Joetta, look at what Joanna's wearing today." I nudged her. Joanna's loose fitting pants outfit was silvery grey with an iridescent shine to the fabric. She wore a square silver necklace with a large rose colored stone set in black metal, all of which highlighted the silver of her hair. I complimented her on her platinum impact and on the necklace. "What a beautiful piece, Joanna."

"Thank-you."

"What type of stone is it?" I asked.

"Rose quartz," she said, lifting the heavy stone from her chest.

"The heart stone?"

"Yes. I love this necklace and usually wear it the last day or so of the retreat. By this time our hearts are more open and I like to believe the stone both contributes to our feelings of love for each other and soaks up the energy here." She laughed and settled the stone against her shimmering shirt.

"This morning," she said, "we'd like to have about half an hour to share, then move into completing the work we started yesterday. This is the next to the last day, so you might talk this morning about any insights you've had."

Joetta raised her hand. "This isn't a classroom—no hands please," Tanya gently reminded her.

"I forgot. I'm so excited 'bout a dream I had last night and I want to be sure I get to talk." Her Texas drawl was more pronounced and her blue eyes sparkled. She was alive. The drawn look of the last few days was gone.

Rebecca and I looked at each other. I raised my eyebrows and she opened her eyes wide for dramatic effect—teasing each other.

"I felt really good when I went to bed last night," Joetta raced on. "I actually felt relaxed and trusting for the first time since I can't remember. I said a prayer as I was going to sleep about being willing to surrender to the highest will and I asked for help in healing myself of this cancer. The next thing I knew I was in a dark tunnel flying along really fast. I couldn't see anything, but I felt loving presences around me, supporting me. I popped out of the tunnel onto a hillside at the bottom of a huge mountain. Wild flowers were everywhere—orange, yellow, rose, and blue, brighter than real life, a million times brighter.

"I wondered where I was and a Being of light appeared before me. I wasn't afraid. I couldn't see a face as there was such a startling white and golden light emanating from and around the head and heart. The Being was clothed in a white robe that floated around it so I couldn't tell whether it was male or female."

As she spoke I felt myself drawn into her dream, almost as if I was participating as she described her experience.

Joetta continued. "The Being communicated with me, I couldn't tell how, yet I understood the message. It asked me if I was ready to lay down my burdens of guilt and shame; if I was ready to release that which wasn't love and step out of the old patterns and into the new. I nodded, trusting that this was the right step for me to take. I was led to an area of the mountain covered with grass and asked to sit quietly and be with myself for a moment. When I was ready to release these burdens I was to signal. Out of rooms within myself I gathered old stuff that no longer served me and placed everything in a pile. I signaled to the Being that I was ready.

"This time I could see and feel huge violet eyes intensely upon mine. I was asked if I was ready to release my old things. I was scared to let go of this stuff because I didn't know what would come in its place. The Being gave me total acceptance to retain or let go of the burdens. I nodded that I was ready and stood and said: 'I release these burdens willingly and I give thanks for the lessons they have helped me to learn about myself and others. I forgive myself for any pain I have caused myself or others on this journey, and I trust that all that comes next is only that which is for my highest good.'" As Joetta described forgiving herself, her posture straightened and tears began to fall. She was there again, in the dream.

"We started moving up the mountain. At the top of the mountain, the Being moved to stand just behind me and I felt powerful and at one with myself and the world. I still feel that peace in every cell of my being. Next thing I knew I was back in the tunnel, then awake.

"That was at 4:00 a.m. and I couldn't go back to sleep. I don't know if the cancer's gone, but when I get back I'll see my doctor. Even if it's not gone, I know I'll be able to deal with whatever is in store for me. Well, that's it. I just had to share it with y'all." Joetta gave her radiant smile and beauty to us and I felt blessed.

"What a fantastic dream. But, you don't think it was real, do you?" Donna asked, ever the skeptic.

Joetta was beaming. "I don't care if it was or not. I feel different. I was so loved in that dream and that's what I want every single day." She met Donna's eyes and winked at her.

With a shrug, Donna's expression changed from one of ready-to-do-combat to puzzled. "What am I missing?" she said softly to Rachel, next to her.

"I don't think I can explain it to you, Donna," Rachel said.

Ruth laid her hand on Joetta's. "I don't care if it was real or not either because I see the change in you. I've been worried about you. Thank-you for sharing your dream with us and for sharing you with us. You are a sweet, dear young woman and I'm so glad you've been part of this retreat."

"Thank-you, Ruth. I'm glad I came also. My life has been changed."

"So maybe you can tell us what the Greatest Change of All is?" Donna said, watching Joetta intently.

Joetta closed her eyes and thought for a moment. "I believe for me, it's trusting again in life. Knowing that the suffering I've been through has a purpose, not to punish me, but to help me learn about love and my purpose in being alive. I don't know if this is the Greatest Change of All for you, but I think it is for me."

Tanya walked over to Joetta. "What I have come to know," said Tanya, "is that we often try to run away from life, especially the dark sides. Emotional pain, our so-called sins or character defects are parts of the shadow. It's so important to go deeper into the wounds and fears and then out the other side. Thank-you for being

201

courageous enough to share your pain and healing with us." She gave Joetta a big hug and kissed her on the cheek.

Joanna stood, ending the morning session. Her hair glinted silver in the light coming through the windows behind her and gave the illusion of a halo. It was mesmerizing.

We spent the next hour or so doing shadow work with Gloria.

Rachel cleared her throat. "Can I say something before we break?" She had our attention. "It seems to me that what I've been doing all week is changing my perceptions. I came here to be with other women and get a break from the routines of life. I've certainly accomplished that." She laughed and rolled her eyes.

"But, it's been a lot more. The first exercise of introducing ourselves with a movement began a change in me. I feel more accepting of myself, of my inadequacies, of whatever wounding I brought with me out of my childhood. I don't know that this is the *Greatest* Change of All, but it's a big change for me. I'll have to wait and see how I'm able to maintain this shift at home."

She looked out the window a moment. "Ah. . . you know what it is, I'm more aware of how the parts of my life fit together. I've been fragmented over the last few years as we added children to our relationship. I kept working and having less and less time for myself.

"One change I'll be bringing home with me is more quiet time every day. I'm not sure how I'll accomplish that. I might have to ask Ron to help me with the children more in the evening, but I feel very determined to keep some of what I've found here this week."

Laila nodded, "I don't know what the Greatest Change is yet, but the change I've made so far is realizing how important other women are to me. That feels very significant."

"I've had a good time, for the most part, but, with all respect, I don't think what you've described is the big event I've been looking for this week." Donna was leaning back in her chair, hands clasped behind her head.

Joanna broke in. "Tomorrow is our last day. I promise we won't let you leave here without knowing. Anyone else?"

"I want to respond to Laila's talking about her connection with other women." I turned towards Laila. "You know I live in the Central Valley. For years I hated Lindston." I wrinkled my nose. "Then, a few years ago, five women and myself, formed a women's group. This group is the lifesaver that keeps me afloat in a community where I'm otherwise very out of sync. Maybe you and Ruth can form a women's group when you go back home as a way to support what you've gained here."

"That's a wonderful idea." Laila was thrilled. "Ruth, what do you think?"

"Yes. Let's do it. How do we find the right women?"

"I'll share how ours formed and you can go from there. A couple of us were interested in forming a group and got together to discuss it. We began with eating, of course! A light pasta with a scrumptious salad, as I recall. We had a couple of glasses of wine and laughed hysterically. As soon as I met Rebecca, I knew I'd found a friend. We each thought of one person we might like to have in the group and purposely kept it to six to keep it intimate. We started meeting once a month and it just evolved. I don't think I've missed a meeting since we began. In the last year we've added two women, but only with everyone's agreement. We have the best time together!"

"What a wonderful idea! Thank-you Taylor," Joanna said. "Now, I want to take a few minutes and talk about the shadow work we've been doing. What brave women you are. Facing ourselves is one of humanity's toughest challenges and most of us just don't have the stomach for it. But, pain as well as joy is just part of being human. Shadow work helped me to become more whole. It helped me to go into the deeper aspects of myself and make friends with parts of me I thought were unacceptable.

"Taylor, the work you did to reclaim the innocence of adolescence by acknowledging the pain of the messages you received touched me.

"Joetta, I can tell by looking at you that something profound has happened within you. I don't know if the cancer will be healed or not, but I would say the important learning here is your loving and accepting yourself in a way that few do.

"And, Donna, you briefly exposed the gentle child and then bounced back into your more comfortable stance, and that's O.K.. You're such a delight and you are yourself. I appreciate that I don't have to guess at how you're thinking or feeling. You're just right there with it all. But enough of my observations, how about lunch?" Everyone groaned in relief. Hard work, this growing and changing stuff!

I walked out of the room with Laila on my heels. "Taylor, can I ask you more about your women's group?"

"Sure."

"What do you do, how often do you meet and what's the purpose?"

"Rebecca, help me out here." I pulled my roommate towards us. "We meet once a month," I began, "and when we started we would have it at a different woman's house each time. Now, we usually meet at Rebecca's each time. We socialize when we first come together, catch up on news, events, what each of us is doing. We might bring books we want to share or fliers about workshops we know about. We usually have some kind of snack, and at Rebecca's, it's often something chocolate," I laughed.

"Who me?" Rebecca said.

"Then usually about an hour before we finish we meditate. It's interesting, the energy when we come together is very high, lots of greeting and laughing and joy at being together. Meditating in a group increases the energy. It reminds me of that saying that I believe comes from the Bible, 'when two or more come together. . . ' Sometimes, before we meditate, we include the names of people we know who need healing, or projects we would like group support for, such as the violence in different parts of the world.

When we've finished meditating we share if we had any particular insights or awareness's of the people we included. Some of our members are incredibly visual, like Linda, and we all have such fun when she shares some of her journeys. I tend to feel energy more than see images. We usually include healing the planet in some way during our meditations also. Once we've meditated we wrap up within half an hour. Did I leave anything out, Rebecca?"

"You didn't say anything about the barely dressed men we have serving the chocolates."

"You're right, I forgot to mention that."

Laila knew us well enough to see the grain of truth here. "You're kidding, right?"

"Well, it's something we're seriously thinking of adding," Rebecca grinned.

"It sounds wonderful. I hope I can pull one together at home," Laila said. "And maybe I will have men servants!"

"I'm so glad you're going to do this," I said.

Rebecca added. "You'll love it, Laila."

"It just feels like the right time. And, I know Ruth will join. I can think of a couple other women that might be interested. I'll let you know."

"I'd love that." I gave her a big hug as did Rebecca and we headed off to our room to get coats.

"Let's eat and then take a walk by the ocean. I need to smell the sea air. Are you game?"

"Yes!" Rebecca gave a little leap.

Chapter 19

I took off my shoes, set them out of the water's path and wandered over to my friends, sand squishing between my short fat toes. My girlfriends were leaning around a circle, absorbed in something.

"Look at these beautiful starfish!" Rebecca pointed as I joined them and looked down. There were six of them roughly in a circle. "Makes me think of our women's group. Synchronicity. These six starfish could have some meaning for us. I wonder what that meaning might be?" Rebecca was pondering the potential significance when Donna stepped in.

"Oh good grief. There's no particular meaning in these starfish. They're here, there's six of them. So what?" She said, ready for war as usual.

"O.K., O.K.. You're both right," Rebecca grumbled.

"Well, for me, it's more fun to play with the possibilities. But, I can see your point Donna. Can you see ours?" I asked.

Donna stirred the circle with her bare toe. "You mean, these six starfish might have some deeper meaning, because we happen to be here and in ten minutes we would have missed it, because the ocean would have washed them away?" Hands on her hips now. "Oh, I suppose I can see it, I just don't believe it. Reality is fine with me."

"This is reality! They're here and we're here." Now Linda had her hands on her hips and her face was flushed. "And, isn't this the way life is? Events happen and we interpret them according to how we believe. It's fascinating. Who believes this is a synchronous something, and who sees it more practically?"

"I'm for fantasy," Rebecca quipped.

"Me too," said Linda raising her hand.

"You know where I stand, Taylor," Donna said.

"I can see both, but if I had to, I'd choose synchronicity," I said. "Know why? Because the mystery of life is more fun! I'm here on this beautiful beach with my best friends and it feels more rich and carefree to see the mystery that these starfish represent."

Donna and Linda looked at each other and laughed. "You sure keep me on my toes," Donna said. "I guess I get awfully linear and feel like I have to protect my intellectual territory. I'd like to let go of that need to protect myself that I have at work. Know what I mean?" We all linked arms and walked back to the car, close and comfortable—my girlfriends.

As we pulled into the driveway and parked the car Rebecca and I said in unison, "I'm so excited about tomorrow." We laughed and as we all moved toward the house, we stopped. The groomed grounds, immaculate flower beds and delicate aromas wafting around us as the sun set, was overwhelming. I closed my eyes and filled my lungs.

"What a week. I feel blissed out with all this love, friendship, beauty, and food, of course!" I smiled at my friends as we said goodnight.

In my bed, with the covers pulled up around me, I felt very grateful for the time and opportunity to be at this retreat. I sent blessings and prayers out to the world and drifted off to sleep wondering what the last day of the retreat would bring.

Chapter 20

I climbed out of a foggy sleep to the rustlings of Rebecca. I opened my eyes and peeked out. She saw me. "O.K., Sunshine, time to get up." She was dressed, hair and make-up done and ready for the day.

"What time is it? You look like you've been up for hours."

"I'm ready for the Greatest Change, aren't you?"

"In forty-five minutes I will be," I said scrambling out of bed and heading to the bathroom. "Are you packing now or later?"

"Honey, I'm packed!"

"Oh, I'm inadequate. I'll pack later. Thank God for earplugs. I didn't even hear you being so efficient this morning."

She headed out the door and I plunged into my morning bathroom routines. Forty-minutes later with stomach grumbling, I made my way to the dining room.

Everyone was already eating. It was nine o'clock— later than I'd realized. We were scheduled to finish the day's activities by 2:00 to give people time to get home. The air was charged with anticipation about the completion of our journey together.

I got my breakfast tray and picked among the fresh fruits for the choicest strawberries. I piled them onto granola covered with light milk and a touch of cream and brown sugar. I balanced a cup of coffee on the tray and joined the table with Ruth, Rachel and Veronica.

"Good last morning you beautiful women!" I said, sliding my tray down next to Veronica.

"Hi! We were talking about our dreams from last night. Did you have any?"

"I slept so soundly I don't remember a thing. You?"

"I had a dream so beautiful and powerful I didn't want to wake up," Veronica said. "I was a doctor, but I worked in a healing center with other physicians, therapists, massage therapists and healers. There was a large meditation room for clients and staff. Taylor, you were there, and Rebecca and Linda. The atmosphere was something. Music everywhere. There was aromatherapy and color therapy. I could see myself asking for guidance and healing for the patient's highest good in the meditation room. I didn't want to leave at the end of the workday because I was so charged and happy. I wonder if it's possible to have this type of a healing center?" Veronica sighed and looked at us.

"It sounds incredible!" Ruth said. "A doctor who wouldn't just push pills. I'd love that! I'll bet there's lots of doctors who would be interested in starting an alternative healing center."

"Taylor, would you be interested in helping me investigate an alternative healing center?"

"You know I love aromatherapy and believe there have got to be better ways of treating physical illness. And, I've felt frustrated over the years with talking therapy. I think some talking therapy is great because I believe some people have a need to tell their story and have it witnessed. I also think some people are so lonely and isolated they just need the caring contact of at least one person until they're able to find a loving circle of their own. But, yes, I'm interested. Only right now, I'm more interested in the Greatest Change of All." I held up a luscious red ripe strawberry for all near me to admire, then slid it into my mouth. . .ahhh!

"Isn't it possible that part of the Greatest Change is exploring and implementing other forms of healing?" Veronica was unwilling to let her healing center go.

"Of course. But, I think the healing center is something that will come out of the Greatest Change and that first we must know what it is," I emphasized.

"I feel so alive being here with all of you during this week. I'm really going to miss you Taylor and Veronica," Rachel told us.

"Well, then, let's keep in touch. I love to write and talk on the phone," I told her. "Write down your phone number, home and e-mail address for me."

Laila came over and stood near Ruth's chair. "Sounds like you're having fun over here. I can't wait to know more about the Greatest Change, but I'm sad about leaving this beautiful place and all of you."

"I was just saying the same thing," said Rachel as she stood up and put her arm around Laila.

"Yes," I said. "This has been an incredible week and I know all of you will be in my heart forever."

The other women had begun to clear their dishes and make their way to the meeting room. Ruth, Laila, Rachel, Veronica and I followed silently. My stomach was nervous and excited, like it would be if I was about to give a speech that I felt unprepared for.

I thought back to the beginning of the week. In such a short time we had developed a wonderful closeness and sense of love for each other. We would probably never come together as a group again and I cherished the intimacy. I was also thinking of Jim, the pull of home and my desire for him. I fiddled with the soft silky material of my blouse and warmth crept up my chest toward my cheeks.

Self-consciously, I looked over at Joanna and Tanya. Joanna's hair was up in a bun secured with a silver Mexican comb. Tanya's blonde waves were loose and long. Joanna wore blue silky pants with a billowy white blouse. Tanya had on white shorts with a knit short-sleeved top. Wild colorful earrings almost touched her shoulders as they played hide-n-seek with her hair.

The air in the room was electric!

I turned to Rebecca, on my right. "Let's get on with it." She nodded.

Tanya stood. "Good morning," she said. "You all appear very excited this morning. I'll share the breakdown of this last day's events. First, we'll discuss what we've learned this past week and then make more clear what the

Greatest Change of All is, though Joanna and I believe you know more than you're aware of at this point." She smiled a big, mysterious smile. "We'll end by honoring the Altar we birthed at the beginning of the week and by dismantling it as we say goodbye to it and to each other. Any questions?"

No one said anything. Joanna, from her seat on the floor, said, "Let's have an informal discussion, in no particular order, of what you've learned and experienced for yourselves this week. One of us will write the salient comments on the white board. I'd like to ask you to take a couple of moments and close your eyes and breathe and go within and allow your Highest Selves to be present to give guidance and direction for this discussion. Go ahead and do that at your own pace." She closed her eyes and began breathing deeply. Tanya lowered the volume of music in the background. . . .

After a few moments Joanna called our attention back to the room. "When you're ready please share."

"I feel so different today than when I walked through the door barely a week ago, I can hardly believe I'm still me," Joetta began. She was calm, her voice low. "My need for self love, deeper friendships and spiritual connection are clear. I think when I go back home I'll start going to church again. I don't know if the spiritual connection I'm needing is going to be fulfilled in a church, but I'll start there and see what happens. I know I have more healing to do with this cancer, but I'm not at the mercy of it any more," she drawled as tears sprang to her eyes. "This is the Greatest Change of All for me, this sense of me I feel I never had before. Thank-you all so much."

Joetta looked each of us in the eye as she gazed steadily around the circle.

Tanya had written on the board:
aware of who I am
connection to self and others
spiritual connection.

There was a pause as we invisibly sensed who would speak next. Rebecca broke the silence. "I've been very aware of my need for quiet time this week. I get so caught up in my social life and the needs of family and clients that I forget me. This week has given me the gift of time for me and only me. The Greatest Change of All is about love—it must be love. I love all of you and just thank you for being here and being who you are." She, like Joetta, had tears in her eyes as she finished.

I looked at the board. Joanna had written:
love and appreciation for
the blessings in our lives

Ruth then began, "In the earlier part of the week I was so angry with Taylor for what I saw as lack of caring about Joetta. I guess my definition of caring has to change. I was raised to believe that caring meant doing something for someone, fixing or taking away pain and what you said about detaching and allowing made me crazy. I thought, 'Taylor's just a bad therapist—I'd never go to her.' It seemed as if others felt the same about this detaching thing. I felt confused as the week wore on. I'm not totally convinced, you understand, but I can see that perhaps my brand of caring has something to do with control." She looked down at her hands and paused. Laila was next to her and reached out and laid her hand on her upper arm and then removed it. "I don't know how to care differently for those I love, but I think I'm willing to try."

"Ruth," Joanna's voice was warm. "Thank-you so much for your honesty about your struggles this week." She wrote on the board:

being honest with ourselves
being willing and open to learn

I looked over at Ruth, whom I'd come to care about. "Ruth, I know it was hard for you. It was hard for me not to back down and say something that would make you feel better. Thanks for hanging in there with me."

The board now reflected:

standing firm and allowing

Linda pushed her hair behind her ears. "I've become convinced during this week that it's O.K. for me to give myself individual time away from my husband and children," she said. "I've never given myself a week away from my family. It's been heaven. I've always felt too guilty to even think about more than a weekend away. How would they survive without me?

"I've only talked with them once this week and they appeared to be doing great. How could they?" she teased. "Could this be the Greatest Change of All?" As Linda finished talking she mouthed "next" to the rest of us.

Joanna added to the board:

time for self

Veronica was sitting cross-legged on the floor, her eyes shining. She was bursting to go next. She cleared her throat and began, "The vision I shared this morning with some of you about the healing center," she paused and gathered her thoughts, "that's why I came to this retreat. Do you believe in synchronicity? I feel clearly that while this has been a wonderful week in many ways, *the* reason I came here was for this vision of the work I am to do sometime in the future."

She shifted her legs and stretched her back. "The other important thing I've learned this week came from the shadow work. The balance of head and heart is really important. My scientist side is left-brained and I've sometimes lost connection with my heart."

Joanna started a new column on the board:

vision
perfect path
balance of head and heart

Speaking next, I said, "I've gained so much during this week but if I had to pick the one or two most important lessons for myself I'd say it was the shadow work. I released more of that old stuck emotional energy I've been dragging around with me for thirty years! It feels so good to let that old shame evaporate and feel more loving and accepting of myself." I smiled at my dear friends. They'd helped more than they knew. "The other thing I got here is the great FOOD!" I raised my right arm in a salute.

Everyone let out a little cheer and now on the board was:

releasing old emotional baggage
Shadow work.

The rest of the women, Rachel, Gloria and Laila reported what they had received from the week. Rachel shared Linda's awareness of how important having individual time away from the family is; Gloria reiterated her hope that in the future her relationships would reflect her contentment with self rather than neediness; Laila stated she realized how important it is to let go of the past and live in the present moment.

Tanya wrote on the board to reflect what the last three women had shared.

There was only one person we hadn't heard from and everyone was quietly waiting to see if and what Donna had to say.

"O.K., O.K.. I can see you're all waiting for me to say I've had some incredible revelation and now my life is changed. But, I didn't have any big metaphysical shift of consciousness. I'm still skeptical of all this *woo woo* stuff.

"I think you're all great women and I like you very much. I have to say one thing I got out of this week is even more of an interest in protecting children. I know my work as an attorney is important. I've always felt it was. But most important is if I can help prevent child abuse in any way.

"I must admit that the work I did with the play-acting, or whatever that was, made me very, very, uncomfortable. As Taylor might say, 'if it's uncomfortable there's probably something there.' I've loved the beauty of this retreat and my walks. I've even gone out a couple of nights and just sat under the stars and appreciated the quiet aloneness. So, this has been a good week." She was quiet, then she looked up and stuck her chin out. "But, I'm not converted."

I laughed. I so appreciate this woman! "I'm glad you haven't lost your skepticism, it keeps me thinking."

Donna shook her head and laughed then turned to Joanna and Tanya and said, "O.K., what's this Greatest Change of All? Are you finally going to tell us?"

They both stood at either end of the white board covered with our discoveries.

"What a wonderful, intelligent, delightful group of women you are," Joanna began. "I just want you to know I've thoroughly enjoyed this whole week and perhaps especially you, Donna. You're so courageous to attend a spiritual retreat when you seem to believe you're so non-spiritual. I think you're quite spiritual and I don't mean that as a dirty word. One meaning for spiritual is 'vital essence' and I'd certainly say you exhibit plenty of 'vital essence' in your presence and, I'm sure, in your work.

"And, I think it's great to have a voice representing the other side. Too often in our culture we focus on the differences and use that to separate ourselves from each other and here I've seen you honor whatever differences there were during our week of living together. I'm sure Tanya feels the same way when I say 'thank-you' for your participation and your courage in your work this week."

Donna took in what Joanna said, but she didn't respond.

Tanya pointed to the board, "Look at what's been written here and just sit for a few moments breathing and asking for guidance about the Greatest Change. See what you come up with."

Donna muttered a "Brother" under her breath as the rest of us gazed and focused our breathing and attention.

I was curious more than anything. All of a sudden, now that it was time for us to understand the Greatest Change of All, I didn't know if it was as significant as I'd been thinking all week.

The ideas that the statements on the board represented floated in my mind and I felt my connection to each of the women. The rhythm of our breathing deepened and synchronized and the air was gently pulsating in response to our attention.

Tanya asked us to keep our awareness open to receive and whenever one of us wanted to share to just do so. We continued to meditate, some with eyes open and some more deeply within. Donna sat quietly as she did when we meditated at home. I often wondered if she didn't get a contact high, such as people who don't smoke pot get when others are smoking in the room.

Someone gasped and I opened my eyes to see who. It was Rachel. "What a mystery life is, what a beautiful mystery. It seems this last week I've been more in the present moment than at most times of my life. I've moved from one experience to another, enjoying each one and letting go of each one to fully experience the current. It reminds me of what you said in the beginning of the change portion of the retreat about children being in the present and flowing from one moment to the next without over-thinking, analyzing or trying to figure out what the next step is. Is this The Greatest Change of All?"

Joanna put her off, "It's definitely part of it. Let's just hold this energy and see what emerges from all of you."

"What I've experienced and learned this last week has been incredible and yet it seems so foreign to what most of the rest of the world believes. Again, I wonder, how I can bring more of this to my everyday life." Laila was troubled. "Is there something I'm missing?"

"Listening to our Higher Self and our connection to the divine instead of always talking or praying or asking for help," I said. "Being quiet each and every day is vital, but, I'm not sure how this relates to the Greatest Change."

"And, let's not forget having fun girlfriends," Rebecca piped in. "This week has been full of learning, but it's also been fun to hang out with all of you. The part I want to take back with me is feeling free like a happy child."

"How much fun is enough?" I teased her.

"That's right, fun *must* be part of the Greatest Change," she said.

"Yeah, so we're getting bits and pieces of the Greatest Change of All, but it still feels like there's something missing," Linda said.

"Keep going," Tanya urged us.

"I don't get it," Donna threw in.

"Yes, I believe you do. All that you're discussing is part of the Change. Keep playing with this." Tanya was pushing us.

What does she want? Suddenly Veronica stood up. "I know!" she said, "I know!"

Chapter 21

"It's a shift of consciousness, isn't it?" Veronica's excitement blazed in her bright eyes. "The Greatest Change of All is a shift of consciousness from the old way of thinking and being to a new paradigm. That's it isn't it?" Joanna and Tanya nodded and smiled.

"Help me out here you two," Veronica said. "It's like it all came together and I could see this is about a paradigm shift. The old model of operating out of our thinking analytical selves is changing. The new model is about operating out of our hearts and minds combined. This is incredible!" She took a deep breath and cleared her throat. "Just think about this, imagine a world that we're now creating where, for example, the center I was talking about earlier comes to mind, where people are able to live out of the wholeness of who they are. Now it's like we're walking heads and we wonder why there's so much dissonance and violence. So many troubled souls in the world. We need the balance of our mind and our hearts in order to accomplish this. We need to connect with our God, however that is."

We were all bubbling with excitement and questions. Even Donna looked interested.

"Very good, Veronica," Joanna said. "Yes, The Greatest Change of All is a shift of consciousness and this shift has profound implications for each of us as individuals and collectively for our world. But, what is our heart energy?" She looked at each one of us. "Love. Very simple." Joanna turned it back to us.

Laila spoke up. "Well, the old way of thinking has created fear and out of fear, problems. Violence, for one. Does violence come out of thinking too much?" she asked.

"In a way, yes. The old model has been one of power over others. For the last few thousand years, we've been following a male way of being in the world and I'm not saying women don't operate out of this model because we've all been raised in this culture and this world. So, when I say male, I could also say left-brained or intellectual or hierarchical.

"In the new model, we don't get rid of the thinking part of our natures, and we don't get rid of money or power, but we begin to change their definitions and how we use that energy. We must begin to operate out of power from within, and guidance from our Higher Selves. We need to incorporate our feelings into our thinking and make different decisions—decisions that have broad implications." She paused.

"Like what?" Donna demanded.

"The Greatest Change is a shift of consciousness and awareness. It's partly a shift of where we choose to place our attention and our energy. Let's discuss it more, play with the possibilities," Tanya again placed the solution back with us.

I took the floor, "What will the world be like? Will we take better care of our children? Will we be less critical of ourselves and each other? Will we value people over technology? Healing instead of a quick fix of symptoms? How will this change affect the number of prisoners, crime, politics?"

"It's not time for answers yet," Tanya said. "Remember we're just noticing that there *is* a shift. The answers will come with time as we live out of this new awareness."

Linda burst into tears. "Oh, I've been desperate for something big to happen to show me that the self-healing I've done and my work as a healer is the right path. I feel so grateful to have been here this week. I'm so happy I followed my gut instincts and overrode my fear of displeasing my family. Thank-you Tanya and Joanna and all of you."

"So, that's it, the Greatest Change of All is a shift of perception?" Donna looked puzzled. "All I need to do is feel more instead of thinking so much?"

"Not exactly," Joanna said. "Think of the Greatest Change as living out of your Sacred Heart. The Sacred Heart represents balance and the wholeness of who we are. Some of us are too emotional, especially under stress. We can't hold a rational thought. That's not helpful. Others think too much. They lose the connection with themselves and others. In the new model it's not one way over the other. It's a balancing of mind and emotions with the overriding support and guidance from our highest spiritual natures." Joanna placed both her hands over her heart.

Donna was tense. Her eyebrows furrowed, a frown at her mouth. "I'm very intelligent, but I *still* don't understand this. I tend to discount things I'm having trouble with, but I'm willing to try to understand what you're saying."

"Don't try too hard Donna," Tanya said. "This shift of perception is more one of allowing and surrendering than trying. We can support our consciousness shifting with many different forms such as meditation, Yoga, Tai chi, prayer, and so on, but we can't force it. We can't *think* this new change into being, but we can prepare the ground and plant the seeds, then allow nature to take its course. I believe that we don't have a lot of choice about the Greatest Change. It's coming; it has been for hundreds or perhaps thousands of years. It's very exciting and scary to make the choices to participate or not." Tanya, her arms hanging loosely at her sides, appeared relaxed. But energy charged the room.

"So how can we help ourselves make this shift of consciousness?" Rachel asked.

"Many of you are already doing what supports this journey," Tanya said with a smile. "We've done activities this week for practice. I believe some form of meditation is essential because it helps us shift our attention away from the outer world and into our inner world." She looked at me. "Taylor incorporates some type of sit down meditation that works. Others get antsy with sit down meditation and so I would suggest activities like Tai Chi or Yoga or even the martial art of Aikido. These are moving meditations that help you develop internal awareness while doing physical activity in a conscious structured manner. For women, I think Aikido is an excellent way to break out of the victim consciousness that keeps us afraid to walk alone or go out at night or even to live alone. What are some other activities you do or can think of that support going within?"

"Walking or just being in nature," Veronica offered.

Donna agreed. "That's where I feel the most peaceful, too," she said. "I don't believe in God, per se, but I do know the importance of having time in nature to help me de-stress."

Joanna was nodding. "As we learn to understand more about our inner landscape through feelings, meditation, dreams and intuition, we learn to listen more to our Higher Self. Our inner connection deepens with practice and we learn to tune into guidance at any minute of the day. A conscious, aware person, in touch with the essence of who he or she is, is a loving person, and the more of us that heal whatever pain keeps us from loving ourselves fully, the more loving and the less violent our world becomes. This Greatest Change of All is incredibly important for our world, isn't it?" Joanna looked at us.

"This change is going to take forever. It all sounds good here in the safety of this beautiful home among all of you who believe, but I can't imagine trying to discuss the Greatest Change with my parents. Forget it," Gloria complained.

"You're right," Joanna answered. "The best way to support this change is to heal yourselves and focus on

227

your becoming as loving as possible without trying to change anyone else. Let people come to you out of your being models of the new way. Believe me, they will. Like moths attracted to the porch light, you'll find people are curious about the changes they will see reflected in you." Joanna gazed out the window.

"Utopia. You're talking about Utopia," Donna jabbed. "Forget it. That's a nice thought but it's not happening."

"I disagree," interrupted Joanna. "I wouldn't call it Utopia. I would call it evolution. With choice we can decide how we want to evolve. With enough of us choosing to allow the full light and love of who we really are to shine, a critical mass will eventually be reached and this Greatest Change of All will be the reality. I urge you all to hold that dream."

Tanya took over. "Yes and I heard that Taylor and some of the rest of you meet every month to meditate collectively. We really encourage you to form groups in your own communities where you can come together with others of like mind and build your connections. Another important aspect of a group can be a safe place to share your story with each other as you did here. Please, please do this. It's so imperative for the good of everyone!"

Joanna stood up. "It's time for us to finish. Letting go of our time together and this wonderful feeling of connection with you is always mixed for me. I've learned from all of you and I will hold each of you in my heart. Let's go to the Altar and in silence remove our offerings and close the group for now."

She led us over to the Altar. It had serenely presided over our entire week. During the week, those of us who were moved to, had added to our original offering. There were flowers, a moss covered curved stick shaped like a half circle, a large round smooth stone and a few feathers, all artistically woven among the imaginative objects. The Altar looked richer, expanded with the week's learnings, much as I felt looking at it. The energy of the Altar had evolved over the week as had we.

We gathered in a circle and one by one went up, knelt or gave a blessing and removed our things. I stood before the Altar and felt an intense shift of energy and sadness that our week was ending. But I was grateful and sent out a prayer of thanks for what I'd received and a wish of love that many more could experience this.

The table was now bare, draped only with the beautiful silk cloth. Then Tanya removed the cloth also. We silently gave each other hugs and went our separate ways to our rooms.

As I walked down the hallway one last time from the meeting room to my room Rebecca caught up with me. We smiled, but maintained our silence. We went into our room and I began to pack. As we started to leave the room I gave thanks for the beauty of the house and the learning I'd received here.

"It's tough to leave this beautiful place, isn't it?" Rebecca said.

"Yes, but I think I'm ready to get back to reality. How about you?"

"Never."

"Oh, right. We're so lucky to have been here for this week. What do you think about the Greatest Change?" I asked.

She didn't have a chance to answer because by this time we were outside by the van and the others were arriving.

"I think I knew what the Greatest Change was before I came here but I hadn't put it into words yet," Linda said.

"Me too," Veronica added.

"Well, I didn't and I'm not sure I do yet. But, I'll try to stay open to it," Donna said.

We all looked at each other with true surprise.

"Good for you Donna. I think I've seen the Greatest Change!" Rebecca teased her.

"O.K., galfriends, time to head home. Yes?" Gloria urged.

"You have a hot date waiting for you at home Gloria?" I asked.

"Well, I'd like to have, but I'm just ready to go."

We waved to Joanna and Tanya, Laila and Ruth who were all on the porch. Laila and Ruth were staying in Mendocino for a couple of extra days. We pulled out of the driveway and drove back down the hill towards the main highway.

"I can't believe it's over. The week went too quickly. So, what do you think?" I asked everyone.

"It seems too simple in some ways. I wonder how our world will be when more of us are able to live our lives in this more balanced manner. Will we ever find meditating or practicing compassion as exciting as shopping? Is it either/or?" Gloria rolled her eyes and we all laughed.

"When are we going to stop for lunch? I'm starving," I said.

"Here we go again!" Veronica said.

"I want to get home in less than the eight hours it took us to drive here. Can you wait until we get to Santa Rosa?" Linda said.

"Anyone have any snacks? An apple, graham crackers, anything?"

"Quick, give her food," Rebecca demanded.

Everyone started digging through their bags and we shared what we produced; apples, a banana, some crackers and licorice for dessert.

"Hey, this'll work," I said happily biting into an apple.

When we got to Santa Rosa we stopped for hamburgers at a place that had meat as well as veggie burgers, then packed up again and maintained a path toward home.

The conversation turned back to the Greatest Change.

"It's so exciting and we're so lucky to be alive at this time aren't we?" Linda said, starting to turn around and make eye contact with us in the back seat, but catching herself. She laughed and kept her eyes on the road.

"Yeah, but are we supposed to do something to get the message out?" Gloria commented.

"I believe we just keep doing what we're doing. Meditating and sending love to people we know who are in pain or crisis, healing ourselves and most of all having fun," Rebecca said as she asked to share some of my snack goodies.

Linda had put some music on that began to lull us into quiet reverie. My eyes were very heavy. I leaned my head back against the seat and dozed off. When I came back to awareness we were almost home.

"She's alive," Rebecca announced.

"Not quite. I've been out for awhile, haven't I? I must really be comfortable with your driving now Linda. Did I miss anything?"

"Yes, and it's too bad because we discussed how The Greatest Change is going to change the world and, well, you missed out," Rebecca teased.

"Oh well, you'll just have to catch me up later. I'm ready to see my Jim and be home. He said he'd have a tasty meal lined up for me and a nice glass of wine. I can't wait."

"This is the time that's hard for me," Gloria said. "I start feeling anxious at the end of a trip with friends because I know I'm going home alone. Scary even to talk about it here." She looked down. "I'm so happy I've got Mary to greet me."

"Your dog?" Veronica asked.

"Yeah. Remember I got her a couple of years ago? I'm so glad I did. At least there's someone at home happy to see me."

"I'm glad you said something about how you're feeling. Thank-you. I believe you're sharing with us like this is part of the Greatest Change, do you know what I mean?" I raised my eyebrow and waited to see if she understood.

"Yes, I think I do."

"I don't know what you mean," Donna said.

"I shared how I was really feeling, my humanness," Gloria said. "I didn't try to hide my real self from you because I feel safe with all of you. Even safer after the retreat. It just came out, I didn't think about it. I trusted you would support me and not make fun of my vulnerability."

"Hmm. . . interesting. Well, I certainly wouldn't go around telling everyone how I was feeling. It's not safe to do that," said Donna folding her arms across her chest.

"You're right. It's not always, but in our group it is, and as we tell the truth, it's even safer to just be ourselves," Gloria said to Donna.

The freeway signs told us that Lindston was only ten more miles.

"We're almost there, and only six hours! We made great time and I want to thank you because I'm anxious to see my family also," said Linda, accelerating.

Soon we were pulling into Linda's driveway and her husband and children poured out of the front door to greet her. We all hugged and thanked each other for a wonderful time and made our way to our cars.

I drove the five minutes to my home eager to see Jim. Although I didn't miss him terribly when I was at the retreat, I realized again, how lucky I am to have him in my life. When I pulled into the garage he opened the door and walked out to give me a big hug and kiss. After unloading all my stuff we stood in the kitchen. He'd poured us a glass of good Chardonnay. We were both full of our week's activities, eager to catch each other up.

"So, what'd you learn? What's the Greatest Change of All?" he asked me, his arms around my waist.

I hugged him. "I'd give you the details, but if I had to put it into one sentence I'd say it's about remembering that we're great and powerful spiritual beings having a human experience and living daily by that remembrance."

"That's not new." His face fell.

"No, you're right, it's not new and that's part of the point, I suppose. We get so involved in our human drama that we forget what we came here to do—remember who we are as we're living out this human experiment. Remember the dream I had about miracles? I was blissed out because I was asking for miracles for people and I could see how they were touched by the love I was sending. I got immediate feedback and I felt incredible because I was able to share my love with others. Just think what the implications are for our world when more of us get high on being in love with ourselves and sharing that love with others by sending thoughts as energy, knowing that those thoughts have an awesome power of their own."

Jim kissed my forehead. "Let's talk more over dinner. It's ready and I know you're hungry."

I grinned at him. "As a matter of fact!"

The table was set on the back patio with flowers from our garden as a centerpiece. We dished ourselves some food and carried our plates out to the backyard. An hour and a half later, I was still telling Jim about The Greatest Change of All.

Author's Note

This is a fictional story based on my life and my work with the names and places changed.

The story line about Taylor's birth daughter is true. I gave a daughter up for adoption when I was 15. It was a choice made for me by my parents who felt they were doing the right thing. This decision caused me great anguish.

I am searching for my birth daughter. A friend of mine believes we will somehow be reconnected through this book. I have very little information about the family who adopted her. The Private Investigator I hired has come up only with dead ends.

To anyone reading the following information, if you believe you have information that may connect us, I ask that you respectfully make sure it's O.K. with her before you pass anything on to me. Please send to any of the numbers listed on the order form (found on the last page of this book).

My birth daughter was born in the latter part of January, 1968. It was a private adoption through my physician. I don't remember his name nor does anyone else in my family. I lived in Whittier, California, at the time. The doctor was in that general area. I know the adoptive mother was a nurse and the adoptive father an engineer and they had coloring similar to mine: blond, blue-eyed. The hospital was Whittier Presbyterian. My maiden name was Elvgren.

I wish to know this young woman and who she has become. I'd like her to know me and my family. Perhaps we can forge some kind of relationship together. I am very respectful of her relationship with her parents. I trust that if we are to be reconnected the Universe will provide that opening.

Women's Retreats

Offered in a 5 - 7 day format,
The Greatest Change retreat is
structured similarly to the one
described in this book. Subjects
covered: Change, The Shadow, Healing
Your Feminine Self, Visioning Your
Perfect Path and Greatest Change.

Available several times a year in
beautiful, nurturing, tropical settings
such as the Hawaiian Islands, the
Caribbean and Mexico.
Call, fax or write for specific details.

Fax:(209) 544-6438
Voice: 1-(888) 656-GCOA (4262)
Web site: www.gcoa.com

A special thank-you to Gina Designs for allowing the use of her artwork, *Circle of Friends, Fine Friends, Love and Support,* to be incorporated in the cover design.

Gina Designs describes her work as *Metalphysical,* a play on words incorporating the material used in the design of the artwork with the spirit of the work. Visit her website, www.ginadesigns.com to view a selection of art including jewelry, apparel, clocks, picture frames, linens and candle holders.

Also a source for Gina Designs:
Iris Blossom, a retail store
163 E. Main Street
Ashland, Oregon, 97520
(541) 482-8662

To order more copies of this book. . .

Complete the Order Form on the next page.

Order Form

Fax orders . . . . (209) 544-6438

Telephone orders   Call Toll Free I (888) 656-GCOA (4262)
                        Have your Visa or MasterCard ready.

On-line orders . . . . http//www.gcoa.com

Postal orders. . . . . Living in Balance, Lynn Telford-Sahl,
                        1700 McHenry Ave. Ste. 65-B, Modesto, CA 95350

Please send the following:

I understand that I may return any books or tapes for a full refund for any reason, no questions asked.

BOOK: **The Greatest Change of All**
                        Price $14.95 + Shipping   Quantity:_____

AUDIO TAPES:

Food Addiction/Compulsive Eating: Non-Dieting Solutions
Includes: What is Addiction?, Feelings: How to Manage.
                        Price: $10.00 + Shipping   Quantity:_____

Living in Balance:
Includes: Breathing, Guided Imagery
I) Creating a Safe Place 2) Interrupting the Binge Pattern
                        Price: $10.00 + Shipping   Quantity_____

Sales Tax
Please add 7.75% for books shipped to California address
                                                    Tax:_____

Shipping:
$4.00 for first book and $2.00 for each additional.
$2.00 for first tape and $1.00 for each additional.   Shipping:_____
                                                    Total:_____

Payment: Check_____ (Make Payable to: Living in Balance)
Credit Card: Visa_____   MasterCard_____
Card # _____ Exp. date_____

Signature_____

Ship to Name: _____

Ship to address: _____

_____
City   State   Zip

Call toll FREE and order now ●   I- (888) 656-GCOA (4262)